LEAP of FAITH

www.**books**at**transworld**.co.uk/daniellesteel

Also by Danielle Steel

SUNSET IN ST TROPEZ	NO GREATER LOVE
THE COTTAGE	HEARTBEAT
THE KISS	MESSAGE FROM NAM
LONE EAGLE	DADDY
JOURNEY	STAR
THE HOUSE ON	ZOYA
HOPE STREET	KALEIDOSCOPE
THE WEDDING	FINE THINGS
IRRESISTIBLE FORCES	WANDERLUST
GRANNY DAN	SECRETS
BITTERSWEET	FAMILY ALBUM
MIRROR IMAGE	FULL CIRCLE
HIS BRIGHT LIGHT:	CHANGES
THE STORY OF MY SON,	THURSTON HOUSE
NICK TRAINA	CROSSINGS
THE KLONE AND I	ONCE IN A LIFETIME
THE LONG ROAD HOME	A PERFECT STRANGER
THE GHOST	REMEMBRANCE
SPECIAL DELIVERY	PALOMINO
THE RANCH	LOVE: POEMS
SILENT HONOUR	THE RING
MALICE	LOVING
FIVE DAYS IN PARIS	TO LOVE AGAIN
LIGHTNING	SUMMER'S END
WINGS	SEASON OF PASSION
THE GIFT	THE PROMISE
ACCIDENT	NOW AND FOREVER
VANISHED	GOLDEN MOMENTS*
MIXED BLESSINGS	GOING HOME
JEWELS	

*Published outside the UK under the title PASSION'S PROMISE

DANIELLE STEEL

LEAP of FAITH

CORGI BOOKS

LEAP OF FAITH
A CORGI BOOK : 0 552 14639 0

Originally published in Great Britain by Bantam Press,
a division of Transworld Publishers

PRINTING HISTORY
Bantam Press edition published 2001
Corgi edition published 2002

1 3 5 7 9 10 8 6 4 2

Set in 11/15 pt Sabon by
Falcon Oast Graphic Art Ltd.

Corgi Books are published by Transworld Publishers,
61–63 Uxbridge Road, London W5 5SA,
a division of The Random House Group Ltd,
in Australia by Random House Australia (Pty) Ltd,
20 Alfred Street, Milsons Point, Sydney, NSW 2061, Australia,
in New Zealand by Random House New Zealand Ltd,
18 Poland Road, Glenfield, Auckland 10, New Zealand
and in South Africa by Random House (Pty) Ltd,
Endulini, 5a Jubilee Road, Parktown 2193, South Africa.

Printed and bound in Germany by
Elsnerdruck, Berlin.

For the leaps of faith I have taken,
and those who have held the net for me,
my children, whom I live for,
Beatie, Nick, Sammie, Victoria, Vanessa,
Maxx, Zara, Trevor and Todd.

with all my love,

d.s.

LEAP *of* FAITH

Chapter One

Marie-Ange Hawkins lay in the tall grass, beneath a huge, old tree, listening to the birds, and watching the puffy white clouds travel across the sky on a sunny August morning. She loved lying there, listening to the bees, smelling the flowers, and helping herself to an apple from the orchards. She lived in a safe, protected world, surrounded by people who loved her. And she particularly loved running free in the summer. She had lived at the Château de Marmouton for all of her eleven years, and roamed its woods and hills like a young doe, wading ankle deep in the little stream that ran through it. There were horses and cows, and a proper barnyard on the lower property at the old farmhouse. The men who worked the farm always smiled and waved when they saw her. She was a laughing, happy child, and a free spirit. And most of the time, as she wandered through tall grass, or picked apples and peaches in the orchard, she was barefoot.

'You look like a little gypsy!' her mother scolded her, but she always smiled when she said it. Françoise Hawkins adored both her children.

Her son Robert had been born shortly after the war, eleven months after she married John Hawkins. John had started his business, exporting wine, at the same time, and within five years, he had made an immense amount of money. They had bought the Château de Marmouton when Marie-Ange was born, and she had grown up there. She went to the local school in the village, the same lycée that Robert had attended. And now, in a month, he was leaving for the Sorbonne, in Paris. He was going to study economics, and eventually work in his father's business. The business had grown by leaps and bounds, and John himself was amazed at how successful it had become, and how comfortable they were as a result of it. Françoise was very proud of him. She always had been. Theirs was a remarkable and romantic story.

In the last months of the war, as an American soldier, John had been parachuted into France, and broken a leg when he landed in a tree on Françoise's parents' small farm. She and her mother had been there alone, her father was in the Resistance, and had been out at one of the secret meetings he attended nearly every night. They had hidden John in the attic. Françoise had been sixteen then, and more than a little dazzled by John's tall, midwestern good looks and charm. He was a farm boy himself and only four years older than she was. Her mother had kept a watchful eye on them, afraid that Françoise would fall in love with him and do something foolish. But John had been respectful of her, and as much in love eventually as Françoise was. She taught him French, and he taught her English, in their whispered conversations at night, in the pitch black of the attic. They had never dared to light so much as a candle, for fear that the Germans would see them. He had stayed with them for four months, and by the time he left, Françoise was heartbroken over his going. Her father and some of his friends from the Resistance had spirited him back to the Americans, and he had eventually taken part in the liberation of Paris. But he had promised Françoise he would come back for her, and she knew without a doubt that he would.

Her parents were killed in the final days just before the liberation, and she was sent to Paris to live with cousins. She had no way of reaching John, his address had been lost in the chaos, and she had no idea he was in Paris. Long afterward, they learned that they had been within a mile or two of each other most of the time, as she lived just off the Boulevard Saint-Germain, and he never knew it.

John was shipped back to the States before seeing her again, and returned to Iowa. He had his own family worries. His father had been killed in Guam, and he had to take care of his own family's farm with his mother, sisters, and brothers. He wrote to Françoise as soon as he got back, but his letters were neither returned, nor answered. They never reached her. And it was a full two years before he had saved up enough money to go back to France, to see if he could find her. He had been obsessed with her since he left. And when he reached the farm where they had met, he found that it had been sold and was inhabited by strangers. And all the neighbors knew was that Françoise's parents were dead and she had gone to Paris.

He went there next, and used every resource he could think of to find her, the police, the Red Cross, the registry at the Sorbonne, as many local schools as he could visit. And on the day before he was to leave, sitting in a small café on the Left Bank, as though by a miracle, he saw her, walking slowly along the street in the rain, with her head down. At first, he thought it was a stranger who just looked like Françoise, but as he glanced at her more closely, and then ran after her, feeling foolish, but knowing he had to try one last time, she burst into tears the moment she saw him and threw her arms around him.

They spent the evening together at her cousins' home, and he left for the States the following morning. They corresponded for a year after that, and then he finally returned to Paris, to stay this time. She was nineteen, and he was twenty-three by then, and they were married two weeks after he got back to Paris. In the ensuing years, nineteen of them, they had never left each other for a moment. They left Paris after Robert was born, and John eventually said he felt more at home in France than he ever had living in Iowa with his parents. It was meant to be, they always said, as they smiled at each other whenever they told their story. Marie-Ange had heard the tale a thousand times, and people always said it was very romantic.

Marie-Ange had never met her father's relatives. His parents had died before she was born, and both his brothers. A sister had died a few years before, and his other sister was killed in an accident when Marie-Ange was a baby. His only surviving relative was an aunt on his father's side, but Marie-Ange could tell from the way her father talked about her that he didn't like her. None of his relatives had ever come to France, and he had said more than once that they thought he was crazy when he moved to Paris to be with her mother. Françoise's cousins had died in an accident when Marie-Ange was three, she had no grandparents, and her mother had no brothers or sisters. The only family Marie-Ange had were her brother Robert, and her parents, and a great-aunt somewhere in Iowa, whom her father hated. He had explained to Marie-Ange once that she was 'mean-spirited and small-minded,' whatever that meant. They no longer even corresponded. But Marie-Ange felt no lack of family. Her life was full, and the people in it treated her like a blessing and a joy, and even her name said she was an angel. Everyone thought of her that way, even her brother Robert, who loved to tease her.

She was going to miss him when he went away, but Françoise had already promised Marie-Ange that she would take her to Paris to see him often. John had business there, and he and Françoise loved going to Paris for a night or two away. Usually when they did, they left Marie-Ange with Sophie, the elderly housekeeper who had been with them since Robert was a baby. She had come to the château with them, and lived in a little house on the property. Marie-Ange loved to visit her, and sip tea and eat the cookies that Sophie baked for her.

Marie-Ange's life was perfect in every way. She had the kind of childhood that most people dreamed of. Freedom, love, security, and she lived in a beautiful old château, like a little princess. And when her mother dressed her in the pretty dresses she bought in Paris for her, she even looked like one. Or so her father told her. Though when she ran barefoot through the fields, in the dresses and smocks she tore while climbing trees, he loved to say that she looked like an orphan.

'So, little one, what mischief are you up to today?' her brother asked when he came to find her for lunch. Sophie had gotten too old to chase after her, and their mother had sent Robert to find her, as he often did. He knew all her favorite haunts and hiding places.

'Nothing.' She had peaches smeared all over her face, and her pockets were full of peach pits as she smiled at him. He was tall and handsome and blond, like their father, as was Marie-Ange. She had blond curls, and blue eyes, and the face of an angel. Only Françoise had dark hair and big velvety brown eyes, and her husband often said that he wished they had another child, who looked just like her. But there was a lot of Françoise's sense of mischief and fun in Marie-Ange's spirit.

'Maman says it's time for you to come in for lunch,' Robert said, shepherding her like a young colt. He didn't want to admit it to her, but he knew how much he would miss her when he went to Paris. Ever since she could walk, she had been his shadow.

'I'm not hungry,' the child said, grinning at him.

'Of course not, you eat fruit all day. It's amazing you don't get a stomachache from it.'

'Sophie says it's good for me.'

'So is lunch. Come on, Papa will be home any minute. You have to come and wash your face, and put some shoes on.' He took her by the hand, and she followed him back to the house, teasing and playing, and running around him like a puppy.

And when her mother saw her, she groaned at what the child looked like. 'Marie-Ange,' she said to her in French. Only John spoke to Marie-Ange in English, and she was surprisingly proficient, although she had an accent. 'That was a new dress you put on this morning. It's in shreds now.' Françoise rolled her eyes, but she never looked angry. Most of the time, she was amused by her daughter's antics.

'No, Maman, it's just the pinafore that's torn. The dress is still all right,' Marie-Ange reassured her with a sheepish grin.

'Thank Heaven for small favors. Now go and wash your face and hands, and put shoes on. Sophie will help you.' The old woman in the

17

frayed black dress and clean apron followed Marie-Ange out of the kitchen, and upstairs to her room on the top floor of the château. It wasn't easy for her to get around anymore, but she would have gone to the ends of the earth for her 'baby.' She had cared for Robert when he was born, and had been overjoyed when Marie-Ange came as a surprise seven years later. She loved the entire Hawkins family as though they had been her children. She had a daughter of her own, but she lived in Normandy and they seldom saw each other. Sophie would never have admitted it, but she was far more devoted to the Hawkins children than she had ever been to her own daughter. And like Marie-Ange, she was sad that Robert was leaving them and going to study in Paris. But she knew it would be good for him, and she would see him when he came home for holidays and vacations.

John had talked briefly about sending his son to the States to study for a year, but Françoise didn't like the idea, and Robert himself had finally admitted that he didn't want to go so far away. They were a close-knit family, and he had a vast number of friends in the region. Paris was far enough away for him, and like his mother, and sister, he was profoundly French, in spite of his American father.

John was seated at the kitchen table by the time Marie-Ange came downstairs. Françoise had just poured him a glass of wine, and a smaller one for Robert. They drank wine at every meal, and sometimes they gave Marie-Ange a few drops in a glass of water. John had adapted easily and well to French customs. He had conducted his business in French for years, but spoke to his children in English so they would learn the language. And Robert was far more fluent than his sister.

The conversation at lunch was as lively as usual. John and Robert spoke about business, while Françoise commented on various bits of local news, and made sure that Marie-Ange didn't make a mess while she was eating. Although she was allowed to roam the fields, her education had been a formal one, and she had extremely good manners, when she chose to use them.

'And you, little one, what have you done today?' her father asked her, tousling her curls with one hand, while Françoise served him a cup of strong, steaming filtered coffee.

'She's been stripping your orchards, Papa,' Robert said, laughing at her, and Marie-Ange looked from one to the other with amusement.

'Robert says eating too many peaches will give me a stomachache, but it doesn't,' she said proudly. 'I'm going to visit the farm later,' she said, like a young queen planning to visit her subjects. Marie-Ange had never met anyone she didn't like, nor anyone who found her less than enchanting. She was the proverbial golden child, and Robert especially loved her. Because of the seven-year gap in their age, there had never been any jealousy between them.

'You're going to have to go back to school soon,' her father reminded her. 'The vacation is almost over.' But the reminder made Marie-Ange frown. She knew that it meant Robert would be leaving, and when the time came, they all knew it would be hard for her, and for him as well, although he was excited by the adventure of living in Paris.

They had found him a small apartment on the Left Bank, and his mother was going to settle him in before they left him to his studies. She had already sent several pieces of furniture and trunks ahead, all of which were waiting for him in Paris.

When the big day finally came for Robert to leave, Marie-Ange got out of bed at dawn and was hiding in the orchard when Robert came looking for her before breakfast.

'Aren't you going to have breakfast with me before I go?' he asked. She looked at him solemnly and shook her head. He could see easily that she'd been crying.

'I don't want to.'

'You can't sit out here all day, come and have some café au lait with me.' It was forbidden to her, but he always let her take a long sip of his, and what she liked best were the *canards* he let her make, dipping rough lumps of sugar in his coffee until they were soaked through with it. She would pop them into her mouth with a look of ecstasy before Sophie saw her.

'I don't want you to go to Paris,' Marie-Ange said with tears filling her eyes again, as he took her gently by the hand, and led her back to the château, where their parents were waiting for them.

'I won't be gone long. I'll come home for a long

weekend on All Saint's Day.' It was the first holiday he had on the schedule the Sorbonne had sent him, and it was only two months away, but it seemed an eternity to his little sister. 'You won't even miss me. You'll be much too busy torturing Sophie and Papa and Maman, and you'll have all your friends at school to play with.'

'Why do you have to go to the stupid Sorbonne anyway?' she complained, wiping her eyes with hands that were still covered with dust from the orchard, and he laughed when he looked at her. Her face was so dirty she looked like an urchin. She was so pampered and so loved and so protected. She really was their baby.

'I have to go to get an education, so I can help Papa run his business. And one of these days you'll go too, unless you plan to climb trees forever. I suppose you'd like that.' She smiled at him through her tears, and sat down next to him at the breakfast table.

Françoise was dressed in a chic navy blue suit she had bought in Paris the year before, and their father was wearing gray slacks and a blazer, and a dark blue Hermès tie that Françoise had bought him. They made a striking couple. She was thirty-eight years old, and looked a good ten years younger, with a girlish figure, and a lovely, unlined face, and the same delicate features John remembered from the first day he met her. And he was as handsome and blond as he had been when he parachuted over her parents' farmhouse.

'You have to promise you'll listen to Sophie while I'm gone,' Françoise admonished Marie-Ange, as Robert slipped her a dripping *canard* of coffee under the table, and she popped it into her mouth with a grateful look at him. 'Don't go roaming around where she can't find you.' She was starting school herself in two days, and her mother hoped it would keep her mind off her brother. 'Papa and I will be home on the weekend.' But without Robert. It seemed like a tragedy to his little sister.

'I'll call you from Paris,' he promised.

'Every day?' Marie-Ange asked him with the huge blue eyes that were so like his and their father's.

'As often as I can. I'll be pretty busy with my classes, but I'll call you.'

He gave her a huge hug and squeeze and kissed her on both cheeks when he left, and got into the

23

car with his parents. They each had a small overnight case in the trunk, and just before he shut the door, Robert pressed a little package into her hand, and told her to wear it. She was still holding it as the car drove away, and she and Sophie stood side by side, crying and waving. And as soon as she walked back into the kitchen, Marie-Ange opened the gift, and found a tiny gold locket, with a picture of him in it. He was smiling, and she remembered the photograph from the previous Christmas. And in the other half of the locket, he had put a tiny photograph from the same day, of their parents. It was very pretty, and Sophie helped her put it on, and fastened the clasp on the thin gold chain it hung on.

'What a nice present for Robert to give you!' Sophie said, dabbing at her eyes, and clearing the dishes off the breakfast table, as Marie-Ange went to admire the locket in the hall mirror. It made her smile to look at it, and she felt a pang of loneliness again as she looked at her brother's face in the picture, and another as she looked at the photograph of her father and mother. Her mother had given her two big kisses before she left, and her father had hugged her and ruffled her curls as he always did, and promised to pick her up at school at noon on Saturday, when they got back from Paris. But the house seemed empty now without them. She drifted up to Robert's room on the way to her own, and sat on her bed for a while, thinking about him.

She was still sitting there, looking lost, when Sophie came upstairs half an hour later to find her. 'Do you want to come to the farm with me? I have to get some eggs, and I promised to bring some biscuits to Madame Fournier.' But Marie-Ange only shook her head sadly. Even the delights of the farm held no lure for her this morning. She was already missing her brother. It was going to be a long, lonely winter at Marmouton without him. And Sophie resigned herself to going to the farm alone. 'I'll be back in time for lunch, Marie-Ange. Stay in the garden, I don't want to have to look all over the woods to find you. Do you promise?'

'*Oui*, Sophie,' she said diligently. She didn't feel like going anywhere, but once Sophie was gone, she wandered out into the garden, and found nothing to do there. And then she decided to go down to the orchards after all, and pick some apples. She knew Sophie would make a *tarte tatin* with them, if she brought back enough of them in her apron.

But even Sophie was out of sorts when she came back at noon, and made some soup and a Croque Madame for Marie-Ange. It was normally her favorite lunch, but today she only picked at it. Neither of them was in great spirits. And Marie-Ange went back out to the orchard to play afterward, and for a while, she just lay nearby, in the grass, looking up at the sky, as she always did, and thinking of her brother. She lay there for a long time, and it was late in the afternoon when she wandered back to the house, barefoot as usual, and looking as disheveled as she always did by that hour. And she noticed that the car of the local gendarmerie was parked in the courtyard. Even that didn't excite her. The local police stopped by occasionally to say hello, or have tea with Sophie and check on them. She wondered if they knew her parents had gone to Paris. And as she walked into the kitchen, she saw a policeman sitting with Sophie, and noticed that Sophie was crying. Marie-Ange assumed she was telling the officer that Robert had gone to Paris. Just thinking of it made Marie-Ange touch her locket. She had felt for it all afternoon, and wanted to make sure she hadn't lost it in the orchard. And as she walked farther into the room, both the officer and Sophie stopped talking. The old woman looked at her with such desolation in her eyes, that Marie-Ange looked at her, and wondered what had happened. It was more than just Robert, she could sense that. She wondered suddenly if something had happened to Sophie's daughter. But neither adult spoke a word, they just stared at the child, as Marie-Ange felt an odd ripple of fear run through her.

There was an endless pause, as Sophie looked at the gendarme and then the child, and held out her arms to her. 'Come and sit down, my love.' She patted her lap, which she hadn't done in a long time, because Marie-Ange was nearly as big as she now. And as soon as Marie-Ange sat down on her, she felt the frail old arms go around her. There was no way Sophie could say the words, to tell Marie-Ange what she had just heard, and the gendarme could see that he was going to have to be the one to tell her.

'Marie-Ange,' he said solemnly, and she could feel Sophie shaking behind her. Suddenly all she wanted to do was put her hands over her ears and run away. She didn't want to hear anything he was going to tell her. But she couldn't stop him. 'There has been an accident, on the road to Paris.' She could hear her own breath catch, and feel her heart racing. What accident? There couldn't have been. But someone must have been hurt for him to come here, and all she could do was pray it wasn't Robert. 'A terrible accident,' he went on deliberately, as Marie-Ange felt terror rise in her like a tidal wave. 'Your parents, and your brother—' he began as Marie-Ange leaped off Sophie's lap and tried to bolt out of the kitchen, but he caught her and held her fast by one arm. As much as he didn't want to, he knew he had to tell her. 'They were all three killed an hour ago. Their car collided with a truck that spun off the road, and they were killed instantly. The highway police just called us.' His words ended as suddenly as they had begun, and Marie-Ange stood frozen, feeling her heart pound, and listening to the clock tick in the silence of the kitchen. She stared at him in fury.

'That's not true!' she shouted at him then. 'It's a *lie*! My parents and Robert did not die in an accident! They're in Paris.'

'They never got there,' he said mournfully, as a sob escaped Sophie, and at the same moment, Marie-Ange began to cry frantically and wrestle with the powerful hand that held her. Not knowing what else to do, nor wanting to hurt her, he released her, and like a torpedo she flew out of the door and raced in the direction of the orchard. He wasn't sure what to do, and turned to Sophie for direction. He had no children of his own, and this wasn't a task he relished. 'Should I go after her?' But Sophie only shook her head and wiped her eyes on her apron.

'Let her be for now. I will go after her in a little while. She needs some time to absorb this.' But all Sophie could do was cry as she mourned them, and wonder what would happen to her and Marie-Ange now. It was so unthinkable, unbearable, those three lovely people dead in an instant. The scene of carnage the gendarme had described was so terrible, Sophie could barely listen to him. And all Sophie could hope was that it had been painless. All she could do now was worry about Marie-Ange, and what would become of her without her parents. The gendarme had no idea when she asked him that, and said that he was sure an attorney for the family would be contacting them about the arrangements. He could not answer Sophie's questions.

It was dusk when she went out to find Marie-Ange after he left, but it did not take her long to find her. The child was sitting next to a tree, with her face on her knees, like a small anguished ball, and she was sobbing. Sophie said nothing to her, but let herself down on the ground, to sit beside her.

'It is God's will, Marie-Ange. He has taken them to Heaven,' she said through her own tears.

'No, He *hasn't*,' she insisted. 'And if He has, I hate Him.'

'Don't say that. We must pray for them.' As she said it, she took Marie-Ange in her arms, and they sat there for a long time, crying together as Sophie rocked her gently back and forth and held her. It was dark when they went back finally, and Sophie had an arm around her. Marie-Ange looked dazed as she stumbled toward the château, and then looked up at Sophie in terror as they reached the courtyard.

'What will happen to us now?' she asked in a whisper, as her eyes met the old woman's. 'Will we stay here?'

'I hope so, my love. I don't know,' she said honestly. She didn't want to make promises to her she couldn't keep, and she had no idea what would happen. She knew there were no grandparents, no relatives, no one who ever visited from America. As far as she knew, there were no relatives on either side, and Sophie believed, and Marie-Ange felt, that she was alone in the world now. And as she contemplated a future without her parents or Robert, Marie-Ange felt a wave of terror wash over her, and she felt as though she were drowning. Worse than that, she would never see her parents or brother again, and the safe, protected, loving life she had known had ended as abruptly as if she had died with them.

Chapter Two

The funeral was held in the chapel on the property at Marmouton, and throngs of people came from the neighboring farms, and village. Her parents' and Robert's friends were there, his entire class from school, those who had not already left for university elsewhere, and her father's business associates and employees. People had prepared a meal at the château, and everyone came to eat or drink or talk afterward, but there was no one to console except the child they had left, and the housekeeper who loved her.

And on the day after the funeral, her father's attorney came to explain the situation to them. Marie-Ange had only one living relative, her father's aunt, Carole Collins, in a place called

Iowa. Marie-Ange could only recall hearing about her once or twice, and remembered that her father hadn't liked her. She had never come to France, they had never visited or corresponded with her, and Marie-Ange knew nothing more about her

The lawyer told them that he had called her, and she was willing to have Marie-Ange come and live with her. The lawyer would take care of 'disposing' of the château and her father's business, he said, which meant nothing to Marie-Ange, at eleven. He said there were some 'debts,' which was also a mysterious term to her, and he talked about her parents' 'estate,' as Marie-Ange stared at him numbly.

'Can she not continue to live here, Monsieur?' Sophie asked him through her tears, and he shook his head. He could not leave a child so young alone in a château, with only a frail old servant to care for her. There would have to be decisions made, about her education, her life, and Sophie could not be expected to shoulder those burdens. He had already been told by people at John's office that the elderly housekeeper was in poor health, and it seemed best to him to send the child to live with relatives who would care for her, and make the right decisions, however good Sophie's intentions. He said that he would be able to offer Sophie a pension, and was touched to see that it was of no importance to her. She was only concerned about what would happen to Marie-Ange, being sent away to strangers. Sophie was desperately worried about her. The child had barely eaten since the day her parents died, and she had been inconsolable. All she did was lie in the tall grass near the orchard, her eyes staring skyward.

'I'm sure that your aunt is a very nice woman,' he said directly to Marie-Ange, to reassure her. And she only continued to stare at him, unable to say that her father had said his aunt was 'mean-spirited and small-minded.' She didn't sound 'very nice' to Marie-Ange.

'When will you send her away?' Sophie asked in a whisper, after Marie-Ange left them. She couldn't even begin to imagine parting with her.

'The day after tomorrow,' he said, as the old woman sobbed. 'I will drive her to Paris myself, and put her on the plane. She will fly to Chicago, and then change planes. And her aunt will have someone pick her up and drive her to the farm. I believe it is where Mr Hawkins grew up,' he said, to reassure her, but her own loss was too great now to be comforted. She had lost not only employers she admired and loved, and the boy she had cared for since his birth, but she was about to lose the child that she had adored since the moment she first laid eyes on her. Marie-Ange was a ray of sunshine to all who knew her. And no pension would ever compensate her for what she was about to lose now. It was almost like losing her own daughter, and in some ways harder, because the child needed her, and was so open and loving.

'How will we know if they are good to her?' Sophie asked with a look of anguish. 'What if she's not happy?'

'She has no choice,' he said simply, 'it is her only family, Madame. She must live there, and it is a good thing that Mrs Collins will take her.'

'Has she children of her own?' Sophie asked, clutching at some hope that Marie-Ange would find comfort and love there.

'I believe she is quite elderly, but she sounds intelligent and sensible. She was surprised when I called, but willing to take the child on. She said to send her with warm clothes, it is cold there in the winter.' It might as well have been on the moon for all Sophie knew of Iowa. She couldn't bear the thought of sending Marie-Ange away, and vowed to send all the warm clothes she could, and everything Marie-Ange loved in her room, toys and dolls, and photographs of Robert and her parents, so she would at least have familiar things with her.

She managed to fit it all into three huge suitcases, and the lawyer made no comment at the number of bags when he came to pick up Marie-Ange two days later. And as he watched her, he felt his own heart ache. She looked as though she had received such a lethal blow that she was barely able to tolerate or absorb what had happened. There was a look of shock and agony in her eyes, which only grew worse as she sobbed in Sophie's arms, and the old woman looked equally distraught as she held her. He stood there for ten minutes, feeling helpless and uncomfortable as they cried, and then finally gently touched the child's shoulder.

'We must go now, Marie-Ange. We don't want to miss the plane in Paris.'

'Yes, I do,' she sobbed miserably. 'I don't want to go to Iowa. I want to stay here.' He did not remind her that the château would be sold, along with everything in it. There was no reason to keep it, with Marie-Ange being so young and going so far away. Her life at the Château de Marmouton was over, and whether or not he said it, she knew it. She looked around desperately before they left, as though trying to take it all with her. And Sophie was still sobbing uncontrollably as they drove away, and she promised to write to Marie-Ange daily. The car was already gone when the old woman fell to her knees in the courtyard, sobbing in anguish. And after they left, she went into the kitchen, and then back to her cottage, and packed her things. She left it immaculate, and took a last look around, and then she walked outside into the September sunshine, and locked the door behind her. She had already made plans to stay with her friends at the farm for a while, and then she would have to go to Normandy to stay with her daughter.

On the long drive to Paris, Marie-Ange did not speak a single word to her parents' lawyer. He made a few attempts at conversation at first, and finally gave up. She had nothing to say, and he knew that there was little, if anything, he could say to console her. She would just have to learn to live with it, and make a new life with her great-aunt in Iowa. He was sure that in time, she would be happy. She could not remain disconsolate forever.

They stopped for lunch along the way, but she ate nothing at all, and when he offered her an ice cream at the airport late that afternoon, she shook her head and declined it. The blue eyes looked huge in her face, and the curls looked slightly disheveled. But Sophie had put her in a pretty blue dress, with a smocked front, that her mother had bought her in Paris. And she was wearing a little matching blue sweater. She was wearing her best patent leather shoes, and the gold locket that had been her last gift from her brother. It would have been impossible to guess, from looking at her, that she had spent the entire summer running barefoot and bedraggled through the orchards. She looked like a tragic little princess as she boarded the plane, and he stood for a long time watching her, but she never turned to wave. She didn't say anything except a polite '*Au revoir, Monsieur*,' when she shook his hand, and the stewardess led her away to board the plane that would take her to Chicago. He had explained to them quietly that she had lost her entire family, and was being sent to relatives in Iowa. It was easy for them to see that she was desperately unhappy.

The chief stewardess had been overcome with sympathy for Marie-Ange, and had promised to keep an eye on her on the flight, and to get her safely on the next flight once they reached Chicago. He thanked her politely, but it made his heart ache to think of what Marie-Ange had been through. And he was glad that she had a great-aunt at least to take her in and bring her comfort.

He stayed until the plane left the ground, and then went out to begin the long drive back to Marmouton, thinking not only of the child, but of the work he still had to do, disposing of their belongings, the château, and her father's business. And he was grateful, for her sake at least, that her father had left his affairs in good order.

Marie-Ange stayed awake most of the night on the flight, and only after they urged her several times did she pick at a small piece of chicken, and take a few bites of bread. But other than that, she ate nothing, and she said nothing to them. She sat staring out the window through most of the night, as though she could see something there, but there was nothing to see, nothing to dream of now, nothing to hope for. At eleven, she felt as though her entire life were behind her. And when she closed her eyes at last, she could see their faces as clearly as if she had seen them in the locket. She had a photograph of Sophie with her, as well, and her daughter's address. Marie-Ange had promised to write to her as soon as she reached her great-aunt's farm, and Sophie had promised to answer.

They reached Chicago at nine P.M. local time, and an hour later, she was on a flight to Iowa, with her three huge suitcases checked in with the baggage. And at eleven-thirty, the plane touched down in Fort Dodge, as Marie-Ange stared out the window. It was dark outside, and hard to see anything, but the ground looked flat for miles around, and the airport seemed tiny, as a stewardess led Marie-Ange down the steps to the runway, and walked her into the terminal, where a man in a broad-brimmed cowboy hat was waiting. He had a mustache, and serious dark eyes, and Marie-Ange looked frightened of him when he introduced himself to the stewardess as her great-aunt's foreman. Mrs Collins had given him a letter that authorized him to pick Marie-Ange up, and the stewardess in charge of her handed him her passport. The stewardess then said good-bye to her, and the foreman took Marie-Ange by the hand, and went to get her bags. He was startled by the size and number of her bags, and smiled down at her.

'It's a good thing I brought my truck, isn't it?' he said, and she didn't answer. And it suddenly occurred to him that she might not speak English in spite of her American father. All she had said was 'good-bye' to the stewardess, and he had noticed that she had a French accent. But it was hardly surprising, she had grown up in France, and her mother was French. 'Are you hungry?' he asked, pronouncing the words precisely so she would understand him, and she shook her head and said nothing.

He had a porter carry one of the bags to the truck, and he carried the two others, and on the way he told her his name was Tom, and he worked for her Aunt Carole. Marie-Ange listened and nodded, as he wondered if she had been traumatized into silence by her parents' death, or if she was just timid. There was a look of sorrow in her eyes that tore his heart out.

'Your aunt is a good woman,' he said reassuringly, as he began to drive, with her bags in the back of his pickup truck, and Marie-Ange made no comment. She hated her already for taking her away from her home, and Sophie. Marie-Ange had wanted so much to stay there. More than any of them could fathom.

They rode together for an hour, and it was nearly one o'clock in the morning, when he turned off the highway onto a narrow road, and they bumped along for a few minutes. And then she saw a large house loom out of the night at her. She saw two silos, and a barn, and some other buildings. It seemed like a big place to her, but as different from Marmouton as though it had been on another planet. To Marie-Ange, it might as well have been. And when they stopped in front of the house, no one came out to meet them. Instead, Tom took her bags out of the truck, and walked into the farm's old, somewhat dilapidated kitchen, and Marie-Ange stood hesitantly in the doorway behind him. She seemed as though she were afraid of what she would find when she entered. And he turned to her with a gentle smile and beckoned.

'Come on in, Marie,' he said, losing half of her

name. 'I'll see if I can find your Aunt Carole. She said she'd wait up for you.' Marie-Ange had been traveling for twenty-two hours by then, and she looked exhausted, but her eyes seemed huge as she watched him. She jumped when she heard a sound, and then saw an old woman in a wheelchair, watching them from a doorway, with a dimly lit room behind her. It looked terrifying to a child of eleven.

'That's a silly-looking dress to wear to a farm,' the woman said by way of greeting. She had a harsh, angular face, and eyes that were only vaguely reminiscent of Marie-Ange's father's. And she had long bony hands that rested on the wheels of her wheelchair. Marie-Ange was startled to see that she was crippled, and a little frightened by it. 'You look like you're going to a party.' It was not a compliment, but a criticism, and Sophie had packed a great many other 'silly' dresses like it. 'Do you speak English?' the woman Marie-Ange assumed was her great-aunt asked brusquely, as the child nodded. 'Thanks for picking her up, Tom,' she said to her foreman, and he patted Marie-Ange's shoulder encouragingly as he left them. He had kids of his own, and grandchildren, and he felt sorry for the child who had come so far from home, for such tragic reasons. She was a pretty little thing, and she had looked terrified all the way from the airport, despite all his efforts to reassure her. He knew that Carole Collins was hardly a cozy woman. She had never had children of her own, and never seemed interested in talking to them. The children of her employees and friends meant nothing to her. It was an irony that, so late in life, she should find her path crossed with this child. And the foreman hoped it would soften her a little.

'You must be tired,' she said, as she looked at Marie-Ange, once they were alone in the kitchen, and Marie-Ange had to fight back tears, as she longed for the loving embrace of Sophie. 'You can go to bed in a minute.'

Marie-Ange was tired, but more than that, she was finally hungry, but Carole Collins was the first person that night who did not offer her anything to eat, and Marie-Ange was afraid to ask her.

'Do you have anything at all to say?' she asked, looking straight at Marie-Ange, and the child thought it was a reproach that she had not thanked her.

'Thank you for letting me come,' she said in precise, but accented English.

'I don't think either of us had much choice in this,' Carole Collins said matter-of-factly. 'We'll have to make the best of it. You can do chores here.' She wanted to get things straight right from the beginning. 'I hope you brought something more sensible than that to wear,' she said over her shoulder, as she turned her wheelchair around with a practiced hand.

Carole Collins had had polio as a young girl, and never regained the use of her legs, although she was able to drag herself around on crutches with braces on her legs, but she chose not to. The wheelchair was less humiliating, and more efficient, and she had used it for more than fifty years. She had turned seventy that April. She had been widowed when her husband died in the war, and had never remarried. The farm had been her father's, and she ran it well, and had eventually annexed it to her brother's land after he died. John's father had been her brother, and his wife had remarried and moved away, and was only too happy to let his sister buy her out. Carole Collins was the family's only survivor. She knew a lot about farming, and absolutely nothing about children.

She was giving up her spare room to Marie-Ange, and she wasn't pleased about it, although she seldom if ever had visitors anyway. But it seemed like a waste of a good room to Carole, and she led Marie-Ange to it, through the dimly lit living room, and down a long dark hallway, as Marie-Ange followed. She had to fight back tears every inch of the way, from grief, terror, and exhaustion. And the room she saw when Carole turned the light on for her was spare and barren. There was a cross on one wall, and a Norman Rockwell print on the other. The bed had a metal frame, a thin mattress, and there were two sheets and a blanket folded neatly on it, a single pillow and a towel. There was a small closet, and a narrow dresser, and even Marie-Ange could see that there would be nowhere to put what she had brought in her three huge suitcases, but she would have to face that dilemma in the morning.

'The bathroom is down the hall,' Carole explained. 'You share it with me, and you'd better not spend too much time in it. But I guess you're not old enough to do that.' Marie-Ange nodded. Her mother had always liked to take long, leisurely baths, and when they were going out, she spent a long time doing her makeup, and Marie-Ange loved to sit and watch her. But Carole Collins didn't wear makeup, and she was wearing jeans and a man's shirt, and her gray hair was cut short, as her nails were. There was nothing frivolous or particularly feminine about her. She just looked old and grim to Marie-Ange as they looked at each other. 'I assume you know how to make your bed. If not, you can figure it out,' she said with no warmth whatsoever, and Marie-Ange nodded. Sophie had taught her to make her bed long before, although she was never very good at it, and when Sophie would help her, Robert always complained because he had to make his own bed.

The two distant relatives looked at each other for a long moment, as Carole narrowed her eyes appraisingly. 'You look a lot like your father as a child. I haven't seen him in twenty years,' she added, but without much regret, as the words *mean-spirited* leaped to Marie-Ange's mind, and she began to understand. Her great-aunt seemed

47

cold and hard and unhappy, perhaps because she was in a wheelchair, the child decided. But she was polite enough not to ask her about it. She knew her mother wouldn't have wanted her to do that. 'I haven't seen him since he went to France. It always seemed like a crazy thing to me, when he had plenty to do here. It was hard on his father when he left, working the farm, but he didn't seem to care much. I guess he went over there chasing after your mother.' She said it as an accusation, and Marie-Ange had the feeling she was supposed to apologize to her, but didn't. She could see now why he had gone to Paris. The house she was in looked depressing and sad, and his aunt at least was anything but friendly. She wondered if the rest of the family had been like her. Carole Collins was so totally different from her mother, who was warm, and gracious, and lively, and filled with fun, and so very, very pretty. It was no wonder her father had gone to find her, particularly if the other women in Iowa were like this one. Had Marie-Ange been older, she would have realized that what Carole Collins was, more than anything, was bitter. Life had been unkind to her, crippling her at an early age, and then taking her husband from her a few years later. There had been very little joy in her life, and she had none to offer. 'I'll wake you when I get up,' she warned, and Marie-Ange wondered when that would be, but didn't dare to ask her. 'You can help me make breakfast.'

'Thank you,' Marie-Ange whispered, tears bulging in her eyes, but the older woman appeared not to see them. She turned and wheeled away then, as Marie-Ange closed the door to her room, sat down on the bed, and began to cry. She got up finally and made the bed, and then dug into her suitcases until she found her nightgowns, perfectly folded by Sophie. They had little embroideries on them that Sophie had done with her gnarled old hands, and they were of the finest cotton, and like everything else she owned, they were from Paris. Somehow Marie-Ange knew that Carole Collins had never seen anything like them, nor would she ever care to.

Marie-Ange went to bed and lay in the dark for a long time that night, wondering what she had done to have this terrible fate befall her. Robert and her parents were gone, and Sophie along with them, and she was left now with this terrifying old woman in this dismal place, and all she wished as she lay in her bed that night, listening to the unfamiliar sounds outside, was that her parents had taken her with them when they left for Paris with Robert.

Chapter Three

It was still dark the next morning when Marie-Ange's Aunt Carole came to get her. She sat in her wheelchair in the doorway of the room, told her to get up, and then abruptly turned her wheelchair around and rolled herself into the kitchen. And five minutes later, with tousled hair and sleepy eyes, Marie-Ange joined her. It was five-thirty in the morning.

'We get up early on the farm, Marie,' she said, dropping off the second half of her name with studied determination, and after a minute Marie-Ange looked at her and spoke up clearly.

'My name is Marie-Ange,' the child said with a wistful look, in an accent others would have found charming, but Carole Collins didn't. To her, it was

51

only a reminder of how foolish her nephew had been, and she thought the double name sounded pretentious.

'*Marie* will do fine for you here,' she said to the child, setting a bottle of milk, a loaf of bread, and a jar of jam on the table. That was breakfast. 'You can make toast, if you want,' she said, pointing at an ancient, rusting chrome toaster on the counter. Marie-Ange quietly put two slices of bread in it, wishing there were eggs and ham, like Sophie used to make, or peaches from the orchard. And when the toast was done, Carole helped herself to a slice and put jam on it sparingly, left the other piece of toast for Marie-Ange, and put the bread away. It was obvious that her morning meal was a small one, and Marie-Ange was starving.

'I'll have Tom show you around today, and tell you what chores to do. From now on, when you get up, you make your bed, you come in here and make breakfast for both of us, like I just showed you, and you get to your chores before you go to school. We all work here, and you will too. If you don't,' she looked at her ominously, 'there's no reason for you to be here, and you can live at the state institution for orphans. There's one in Fort

Dodge. You'll be a lot better off here, so don't think you can get out of your chores, or working for me. You can't, if you want to stay here.'

Marie-Ange nodded numbly, knowing as never before what it meant to be an orphan.

'You start school in two days, on Monday. And tomorrow we'll go to church together. Tom will drive us.' She had never bought a specially fitted car that she could drive. Although she could have afforded it, she didn't want to spend the money. 'We'll go into town today, after you do your chores, and get you some decent clothes to work in. I don't suppose you brought anything useful with you.'

'I don't know, Madame . . . Aunt . . . Mrs . . .' Marie-Ange groped for her words as her aunt watched her, and all she could think of was the gnawing emptiness in her stomach. She had barely eaten on the plane, and nothing at all the night before, and her stomach was aching, she was so hungry. 'Sophie packed my bags,' she explained, without saying who Sophie was, and Aunt Carole didn't ask her. 'I have some dresses I used to play in,' but all the torn ones she had worn to play in the fields had been left in Marmouton, because

53

Sophie had said her aunt would think them disgraceful.

'We'll take a look at what you brought after breakfast,' her great-aunt said without smiling at her. 'And you'd better be prepared to work here. Having you here is going to cost me a pretty penny. You can't expect room and board for free out of me, and not do anything to pay for it.'

'Yes, Madame,' Marie-Ange nodded solemnly, and the old woman in the wheelchair glared at her as the child tried not to tremble.

'You may call me Aunt Carole. Now you can wash up the dishes,' which Marie-Ange did quickly. They had only used a single plate each for their toast, and a cup for Carole's coffee. She went back to her room afterward, not sure what else to do, and was sitting on her bed staring at the photographs she had put on the dresser, of her parents and her brother. And her hand was touching her locket.

She gave a start when she heard her great-aunt wheel herself into the doorway. 'I want to see what you brought with you in those three ridiculous suitcases. No child should have that many clothes, Marie, it's sinful.' Marie-Ange hopped off the bed and dutifully unzipped her cases, pulling out one smocked dress after another, the embroidered nightgowns, and several little coats that her mother had bought for her in Paris and London. She wore them when she went to school, and for church on Sunday, and to Paris when she went with her parents. Carole stared at them in grim disapproval. 'You don't need things like that here.' She wheeled herself closer to where Marie-Ange stood, and dug into the suitcases herself, and then began making a small pile on the bed of sweaters and pants, a skirt or two. Marie-Ange knew those things weren't beautiful, but Sophie had said they would be useful for school, and Marie-Ange thought now that Carole had put them aside because they were ugly. Without saying a word to the child, she zipped the suitcases up again, and told her to put the things on the bed in the narrow closet. Marie-Ange was confused by what she was doing, and then her Aunt Carole told her to go outside and find Tom so she could learn her chores from him, and then she disappeared to her own bedroom far down the dark hallway.

The foreman was waiting for her outside, and

he took her to the barn, and showed her how to milk a cow, and the other minor tasks that were expected of her. They didn't seem too hard to Marie-Ange, although there were a lot of things her great-aunt wanted her to do, and Tom said that if she couldn't finish in the morning before she went to school, she could do some of the cleaning up in the late afternoon before dinner. It was a full two hours before he returned her to her Aunt Carole.

Marie-Ange was surprised to see her dressed and sitting on the porch in her wheelchair, waiting for them. She spoke to Tom, and not the child, and told him to get Marie-Ange's bags, and drive them into town, as the child looked at her in terror. All she could think of was that she was being dropped off after all at the state institution. And as she followed them to the pickup truck she'd ridden in the night before, she saw the foreman throw her bags behind them into the truck. Marie-Ange said nothing and asked no questions. Her life now was one long, endless terror. There were tears bulging in her eyes as they drove into town, and Carole told the foreman to stop at the Goodwill store. He set up her wheelchair for her, and helped her into it, and then she told him to take the suitcases inside, as Marie-Ange continued to wonder what would happen to her. She had no idea where they were, where they were going, or why they had come here with her suitcases, and her aunt had offered no explanation to reassure her.

The women at the counter seemed to recognize Carole as she wheeled herself inside, and Tom followed with Marie-Ange's bags in both hands, and set them down near the counter, at Carole's direction.

'We need some overalls for my niece,' she explained, and Marie-Ange let out a silent sigh of relief. Perhaps they weren't going to the institution, and at least for the moment, nothing too terrible was going to happen. Her aunt selected three pairs of overalls for her, some stained T-shirts, a worn-looking sweatshirt, and some nearly brand-new sneakers, and they chose an ugly brown quilted jacket that was too big for her, but they said it would be warm in winter. Marie-Ange told them in a soft voice, as she tried things on, that she had just come from France, and Carole was quick to explain that she had brought three suitcases of useless clothes with her, and pointed at them. 'You can take those against what we just bought for her, and give me credit for the rest of it. She's not going to need any of it here, and even less so if she winds up at the state orphanage. They wear uniforms,' she said pointedly to Marie-Ange, as tears began to run down her cheeks, and the women behind the counter felt sorry for her.

'May I keep some of it, Aunt Carole? . . . My nightgowns . . . and dolls . . .'

'You don't have time to play with dolls here,' and then she hesitated for a minute, 'keep the nightgowns.' Marie-Ange dug in one of the suitcases for them, and found them, and as she pulled them out, she clutched them to her. All the rest of it was going to disappear forever, all the things her mother had bought her so lovingly, and that her father had loved to see her wear. It was like having the last of her lost life torn from her, and she could not stop crying. Tom had to turn away from the sight of her, clutching her nightgowns, and looking at her aunt with utter devastation. But Carole said nothing, handed the package of their purchases to Tom, and wheeled herself out of the store and onto the sidewalk, as her foreman and the child followed. Marie-Ange didn't even care now if they took her to the orphanage, it could be no worse than what was happening to her here. Her eyes told a tale of a thousand agonies and few mercies, as they rode back to the farm in silence. And when Marie-Ange saw the familiar barn again, she realized that she was not going to the state institution, not today at least, and perhaps only if she truly annoyed her Aunt Carole.

She went to her room and put away her old nightgowns and new things from the Goodwill store, and her aunt had lunch ready for her ten minutes later. It was a thin sandwich of ham on bread, with neither mayonnaise nor butter, a glass of milk, and a single cookie. It was as though the old woman begrudged her every bite of food she ate, every crumb she cost her. And it never occurred to Marie-Ange to think of the hundreds of dollars of credit Carole had just gotten at the Goodwill store in exchange for Marie-Ange's wardrobe. In fact, for the moment at least, Marie-Ange was profitable, rather than costly.

For the rest of the day, Marie-Ange went about her chores, and didn't see her aunt again until dinner, and that night the meal was spare again. They had a tiny meat loaf Carole made and some boiled vegetables that tasted awful. The big treat for dessert was green Jell-O.

Marie-Ange did the dishes afterward, and lay awake in her bed for a long time that night, thinking about her parents, and everything that had happened to her since they died. She could no longer imagine another life now, except one of terror, loneliness, and hunger, and the grief of losing her entire family was so acute that there were times when she thought she couldn't bear it. And suddenly, as she thought about it, she understood exactly what her father had meant when he called his aunt mean-spirited and small-minded. And she knew that her mother, with all her joy and love and vivaciousness, would have hated Carole even more than he did. But it did her no good to think of that now. She was here, and they were gone, and she had no choice but to survive it.

They went to church together the next day, driven by Tom again, and the service seemed long and boring to Marie-Ange. The minister talked about hell and adultery and punishment, and a lot of things that either frightened or bored her. She nearly fell asleep at one point, and felt her great-aunt shake her roughly to rouse her.

Dinner was another grim meal that night, and her great-aunt informed her that she would be going to school in the morning. Carole had been relieved to realize that although she had a notice-able accent when she spoke, Marie-Ange's English was certainly fluent enough for her to go to school and follow what they were saying to her, although Carole had no idea if she could write it, which she couldn't.

'You walk a mile down the road, to a yellow sign,' she said before they went to bed, 'after you do your chores in the barn, of course, and the bus will pick you up at the yellow sign at seven. It's forty miles to the school, and they make a lot of stops along the way. I don't know how fast you walk, but you'd better leave here at six, and see how long it takes you. You can do your chores at five, and you'd better get up at four-thirty.' She gave her an ancient half-broken alarm clock for that purpose, and Marie-Ange wondered if it came from the Goodwill store. It had been full of tired, broken, ugly things that people had sent there. 'The bus will drop you off after school around

four, they told me. And I'll expect you here by five.
You can do your chores when you get home and
your homework after dinner.' It would be a long
day, an exhausting routine, a life of drudgery and
near slavery. Marie-Ange wanted to ask her, but
didn't dare, why Tom couldn't drive her. Instead,
she said nothing, and went to bed in silence that
night after saying good night to her Aunt Carole.

It seemed only moments later when the alarm
went off, and she got up quickly. And this time,
with no one to see what she did, she helped herself
to three slices of toast, with jam, and prayed that
her aunt hadn't counted the number of slices left
in the loaf when she put it away after dinner. She
knew it was excessive, but she was always hungry.

It was dark when she went outside and walked
to the barn, and still dark when she headed down
the road in the direction that her aunt had told
her. She knew Carole would be up by then, but
Marie-Ange didn't stop in the kitchen to say good-
bye. She was wearing a pair of pants and the ugly
sweatshirt from the Goodwill store. Her hair was
brushed, but for the first time in her life, as she left
for school, there was no ribbon in it. There was no
Sophie to wave her off, no Robert to make

canards of café au lait for her, and no kiss or hug from her mother or father. There was only the silence of the Iowa plains, and the darkness, as she headed down the long, lonely road toward the bus stop. She had no idea what the school would be like, or the children there, and she didn't really care. She couldn't even begin to imagine having a friend here. Hers was the life of a convict, and her aunt was the jailer.

There were half a dozen children at the bus stop when she arrived, most of them older than Marie-Ange, and one considerably younger, and none of them spoke to her. They just stared at her as they waited, and the sun came up slowly, and reminded her of mornings in Marmouton when she had lain in the grass or under a tree, watching the sky turn pink at dawn. She said nothing to the other kids as they took their seats and the bus took off, and an hour later, they arrived at a long, low, brick building, where other school buses had converged, and students were spilling out everywhere, of all ages. They went from kindergarten to high school, and came from farms within a hundred miles of the school. Marie-Ange's was by no means the greatest distance. And looking lost, she wandered into the building, and was quickly spotted by a young teacher.

'Are you the Collins girl?' she asked, as Marie-Ange shook her head, not making the connection. 'I am Marie-Ange Hawkins.' They had been expecting a Marie Collins, and it had never dawned on her that her great-aunt would register her under her own name.

'You're not the Collins child?' The teacher looked perplexed. She was the only new student they were enrolling. All the others had started two weeks before, but she recognized the accent instantly, and led Marie-Ange to the principal's office, where a balding man with a beard greeted her solemnly and told her which room to go to.

'Sad-looking little thing,' he commented when she left, and the teacher answered him in hushed whispers.

'She lost her whole family in France, and came to live with her great-aunt here.'

'How good is her English?' he asked with a look of concern, and the teacher said that her home-room teacher was going to test her.

And as they discussed her, Marie-Ange wandered down the hall in the direction she'd been told, and found her classroom filled with children. The teacher was not yet there, and they were a lively bunch, hooting and screaming and throwing paper balls at each other. But no one said a word to her as she sat down at a desk in the back row, beside a boy with bright red hair, blue eyes like her own, and freckles. She would have preferred to sit next to a girl, but there were no empty seats beside them, and no one offered to make room for her.

'Hi,' he said, avoiding her eyes, as she glanced at him, and then at the front of the room as the teacher entered. It took her over an hour to notice Marie-Ange, and then she handed her some papers with questions that were designed to assess her reading, writing, and comprehension in English. It was pretty basic, and Marie-Ange understood most of it, but her answers, when she wrote them, were phonetic. 'Can't you spell?' the boy asked her with a look of surprise when he glanced at her paper. 'And what kind of name is that? Maree-Angee?' He pronounced it strangely, and Marie-Ange looked at him with dignity as she answered.

'I am French,' she explained. 'My father is

American.' She could have said 'was,' but couldn't bear it.

'Do you speak French?' the boy asked, looking perplexed, but suddenly intrigued by her.

'Of course,' she said, with her accent.

'Could you teach me?' She smiled shyly at the question.

'Do you want to know how to speak French?' It seemed funny to her, and he grinned as he nodded.

'Sure. It would be like a secret language, and then no one could understand what we were saying.' It was an appealing idea to both of them, and he followed her outside at recess. He thought her curls and big blue eyes were beautiful, but he didn't say so. He was twelve, a year older than Marie-Ange, but he had been held back a year after he had rheumatic fever. He had recovered totally, but had lost the year in school, and he seemed to take a protective attitude toward Marie-Ange as he followed her around the schoolyard. He had introduced himself by then, and said his name was Billy Parker, and she had told him how to pronounce her name, his first French lesson, and she giggled at his accent when he said it.

They had lunch together that day, and a few of the others talked to her, but he was the only friend she could claim when she got back on the school bus with him. He lived halfway between school and her great-aunt's farm, and he said he would come to see her one day, maybe over the weekend, and they could do their homework together. He was fascinated by her, and made plans for her to teach him French on the weekends. He seemed to like the idea, and she loved the prospect of having someone who could speak French with her.

She told him about her parents and Robert the next day, and the accident, and he looked horrified when she told him about her Aunt Carole. 'She sounds pretty mean to me,' he said sympathetically. He lived with his parents, and had seven brothers and sisters, they had a small farm and grew corn, and had a small herd of cattle. He said he'd come over and help her with her chores sometime, but she said nothing about him to Aunt Carole, and Aunt Carole asked no questions at night when Marie-Ange finished her chores in the barn. Most of the time, they ate dinner in silence.

It was Saturday afternoon, when Marie-Ange saw Billy ride down the driveway on his bike, and hop off with a wave at her. He had told her he might come by, for his French lesson, and she had hoped he would, but didn't think he'd really do it. They were talking animatedly where they stood when a shot rang out, and they both jumped like frightened rabbits, and looked instinctively at the direction it came from. Her Aunt Carole was sitting on the porch, in her wheelchair, holding a shotgun. It was inconceivable to either of them that she had shot at them, and she hadn't, she had fired into the air, but she was looking menacingly at them.

'Get off my property!' she shouted at him, as Billy stared at her, and Marie-Ange began to tremble.

'He is my friend, Aunt Carole, from school,' Marie-Ange was quick to explain, sure that that would solve the problem, but it didn't.

'You're trespassing!' she said directly to Billy.

'I came to visit Marie-Ange,' he said politely, trying not to let either of them see how frightened he was. The old woman looked as though she were going to kill him.

'We don't want visitors, and we didn't invite you. Get on your bike and get out of here, and don't come back. You hear me?'

'Yes, ma'am,' he said, hurrying toward his bike, with a glance at Marie-Ange over his shoulder. 'I'm sorry . . . I didn't mean to make her mad,' he whispered. 'I'll see you at school on Monday.'

'I'm sorry,' she said as loudly as she dared, and watched him disappear as fast as he could down the driveway, as Marie-Ange walked slowly toward her great-aunt's wheelchair, hating her for the first time since she had come here. Until then, she had only feared her.

'Tell your friends not to come visiting you here, Marie,' she said sternly. 'We don't have time for little hoodlums hanging around, and you have chores to do,' she said, laying the shotgun across her lap and looking straight at Marie-Ange. 'You're not going to be hanging around with friends here. Is that clear?'

'Yes, ma'am,' Marie-Ange said quietly, and walked back toward the barn to do her chores. But the attack on them, and the fear she'd caused, had only cemented the bond between Marie-Ange and Billy. He called her that night, and her great-aunt handed her the phone with a grunt of disapproval. She didn't like it, but she didn't object openly to phone calls.

Danielle Steel

'Are you okay?' It was Billy. He had worried about her all the way home, the old lady was crazy, and he felt sorry for Marie-Ange. His own family was large and open and friendly, and he could have friends over after chores, anytime he wanted.

'I'm fine,' she said shyly.

'Did she do anything to you after I left?'

'No, but she said I cannot have friends here,' she explained in a whisper after her aunt left the kitchen. 'I'll see you at school on Monday. I can teach you French at lunchtime.'

'Just make sure she doesn't shoot you,' he said with the solemnity of a twelve-year-old. 'I'll see ya . . . 'Bye, Marie-Ange.'

'Good-bye,' she said formally as she hung up, wishing she had thanked him for the call, but grateful for the contact from the outside world. In the barren existence she led, his friendship was all she had now.

Chapter Four

The friendship between Billy and Marie-Ange grew over the years into a solid bond that they both relied on. Through their childhood years, they became like brother and sister. And by the time he was fourteen, and she thirteen, their friends began to tease them about it, and asked if they were boyfriend and girlfriend. Marie-Ange always insisted they weren't. She clung to him like a rock in a storm, and he called her faithfully every night at her Aunt Carole's. Marie-Ange's life with her remained as bleak and as gray as it had been from the first moment she saw her. But seeing Billy in school every day, and riding home on the bus with him, was enough to keep her going. And she visited his family as often as she could. Being with them was like taking refuge in a warm safe place. She visited them on holidays, after fulfilling her obligations to Aunt Carole. For Marie-Ange, Billy's family was her haven. They were all she had now. She didn't even have Sophie anymore. She had written to Sophie for two years, and was still puzzled by the fact that she had never had a single answer from her. She was afraid that something terrible must have happened to her. Otherwise, Sophie would have written.

In some ways, Billy had replaced Robert for her, if not her parents. And as she had promised to, she had taught him to speak French during lunch and recess. By the time he was fourteen, he was almost fluent, and they conversed with each other in French frequently in the schoolyard. Billy called it their secret language. And her English had improved to the point that she scarcely had an accent. But given her fraternal feelings for him, it was all the more surprising to her when he told her he loved her, one afternoon as they were walking to the school bus. He said it under his breath, with his eyes cast down, and she stopped to stare at him with a stupefied expression.

'That's the dumbest thing I've ever heard,' she

said in answer to what he had told her. 'How can you say that?' He looked startled by her response – it wasn't what he had hoped for or expected.

'Because I do love you.' He was saying it to her in French, so the others wouldn't understand them, and to them, it sounded like a heated argument, as Marie-Ange said, '*Oh, alors, t'es vraiment con!*' She told him he was a jerk, and then she looked at him and started laughing.

'I love you too. Okay. But like your sister. How can you go and mess everything up between us?' She was determined not to let him risk their friendship.

'I wasn't trying to do that,' he said, frowning, wondering if he had said it wrong, or perhaps at an inappropriate time, but they had no other time together. He still wasn't allowed on her great-aunt's farm, and the only time they had together was in school, or on the school bus. Except for her rare visits to his parents' farmhouse. It was even harder for them during the summer, when they weren't in school together. Instead, they would both ride bicycles to a meeting place they had found the year before, and sometimes spent hours by a small stream, sitting there and just talking to each other, about life, their families, their hopes and dreams and their futures. She always said she wanted to go back to France when she was eighteen, and planned to get a job as soon as she was old enough so she could afford to. And once he had said that he wanted to come with her, although for him, the dream was even less likely and more distant.

They rolled along after that, as they had always been, devoted friends and buddies, until the following year in the summer, when they met at their secret hiding place. She had brought a Thermos of lemonade with her, and they had been talking for hours, when he suddenly leaned over and kissed her. He was fifteen, and Marie-Ange had just turned fourteen, and they had been best friends for nearly three years then. And once again, she was startled, when he kissed her, but she didn't object quite as violently as she had the year before. Neither of them said anything, but Marie-Ange was worried, and the next time they met, she told him she didn't think it was a good idea for them to do anything to change their friendship. She told him in her innocent way that she was afraid of romance.

'Why?' he asked gently, touching her cheek with his hand. He was growing into a tall, handsome young man, and sometimes she thought he looked a little like her father and brother. And she loved to tease him about his freckles. 'Why are you afraid of romance, Marie-Ange?' They were speaking English, because hers was still far superior to his French, although she had taught him well, and he even knew all the important slang expressions, which he knew was going to impress his French teacher in high school. They were both starting high school, at the same school they'd been at, in September.

'I don't want anything to change between us,' she said sensibly. 'If you fall in love with me, one day we will be tired of each other, and then we will lose everything. If we stay only friends, we can never lose each other.' It was not entirely unreasonable, and she remained firm about it, although no one who knew them would have believed that. Everyone had always believed that they were boyfriend and girlfriend since their childhood, even Aunt Carole, who continued to make disparaging remarks about him, which always made Marie-Ange angry, although she said nothing to her.

Danielle Steel

Their relationship continued to flourish all the way through high school. She watched him play on the basketball team, he came to see her in the junior play, and they went to their senior prom together. With the exception of a few random dates, he had never had a girlfriend, and Marie-Ange continued to say she had no interest whatsoever in romance, with Billy or any other boy, all she wanted was to finish school, and go back to France one day. And her great-aunt wouldn't have let her go out with boys anyway. She had strong opinions about it, and was prepared to enforce them. She had continued to threaten Marie-Ange with the state orphanage for all the years she'd been there. But on prom night, Aunt Carole finally agreed to let Marie-Ange go to the dance with Billy.

He came to the farm the night of the senior prom, in his father's truck, to pick her up. And Aunt Carole had let her buy an ice blue satin dress that was almost the same color as her eyes, and made her blond hair seem to sparkle. She looked beautiful, and Billy looked appropriately dazzled.

They had a great time that night, and he and Marie-Ange talked endlessly about the scholarship she had earned, and which she was not able to use, for college. The university was fifty miles away, in Ames, and Aunt Carole had made a point of saying she would do nothing to help her, she would not lend her a truck or a car, and said she was needed on the farm. She offered her neither money nor transportation for college, and Billy was outraged.

'You *have* to go, Marie-Ange! You can't just work for her like a slave for the rest of your life.' Her dream had been to go back to France at eighteen, but it was obvious that when she turned eighteen that summer, she was not going to do that. She had no money of her own, and never had time to work, because Carole always needed her to do something, and Marie-Ange felt obligated to her. She had lived with her for seven years, and to Marie-Ange, they had seemed endless. But college was now an unattainable dream for her, the scholarship covered tuition, but not books, or dormitory, or food, and even if she got a job, she couldn't make enough to cover her expenses while she went to school. The only way she could go was if she stayed on the farm with her aunt, and commuted. But Aunt Carole had seen to it that that couldn't happen. 'All you need is a car for chrissake,' Billy raged on the drive home. They had talked about it all evening.

'Well, I don't have one. I'm going to turn the scholarship down next week,' Marie-Ange said matter-of-factly. She knew that she had to get a job eventually, locally, so she could make enough money to go to France, but she had no idea what she'd do when she got there, probably just visit and come back. She had no way of staying in France either, nowhere to live, no one to live with, no way of making a living. She had no skills whatsoever, and no training. All she had ever learned was how to do chores on the farm, not unlike Billy, who was going to be taking agricultural extension classes. He had dreams of helping his father on their farm, and even modernizing it, despite his father's resistance. He wanted to be a modern-day farmer, and he thought Marie-Ange deserved a real education. They both did. It made him hate Marie-Ange's great-aunt all the more for not letting her go to college. Even his father understood the importance of taking classes, although he couldn't go to school full time. His father needed him too much on the farm to allow him to do that. He urged Marie-Ange to work on her great-aunt some more, and not turn the scholarship down until later in the summer. And as they drove home that night, they were in good spirits. They were both excited about graduating from high school.

'Do you realize we've been friends for nearly seven years?' Marie-Ange said proudly. Her parents had died seven years ago that summer, and in some ways, it still seemed like minutes, in others aeons. But she still dreamed of them and Robert at night, and she could still see Marmouton in her mind's eye as though she had just been there. 'You're the only family I have,' Marie-Ange said to Billy, and he smiled. They both entirely disregarded her Aunt Carole, although Marie-Ange always said that she felt indebted to her, for reasons that escaped Billy. Marie-Ange had lived with her, but Carole had used her mercilessly for the past seven years, as maid, nurse, and farmhand. There was nothing Marie-Ange didn't do for her. For the past two years, her great-aunt's health had been failing. Marie-Ange had to do even more to assist her.

'You know, we could be family permanently,'

Billy said cautiously on the drive home from the prom, and glanced at her with a gentle smile, but Marie-Ange was frowning. She never liked it when he talked that way, and doggedly continued to think of them as brother and sister. 'We could get married,' he said bravely.

'That's stupid, Billy, and you know it,' she said bluntly. She never encouraged him in that direction, for his own sake, as well as her own. 'Where would we live if we got married? Neither of us has a job, or any money,' she said matter-of-factly.

'We could live with my parents,' he said softly, wishing he could sway her. He had just turned nineteen, and she was turning eighteen shortly, old enough to be married, if she wanted, without her aunt's permission.

'Or we could live with Aunt Carole. I'm sure she'd love that. You could work for her on the farm, as I do,' Marie-Ange said, and laughed then. 'No, we can't get married,' she said practically. She didn't want to. 'And I'm going to get a job, so I can go back to France next year.' The dream never died for her, and he still wished he could go with her. In Iowa, working on his father's farm, his

French was virtually useless, but he was happy she had taught him.

'I still want you to go to college in the fall. Let's see what happens,' he said with a look of determination.

'Oh yes, an angel will fall on me from Heaven,' she laughed at him with good humor, as she had adjusted to not going, 'and he will throw money at my feet, so I can go to the university, and Aunt Carole will pack my bags, and blow kisses at me when I leave. Right, Billy?' She had been resigned to her fate since she'd come here.

'Maybe,' he said, looking thoughtful. And the next day he began work on a special project. It took him all summer to do, and his brother helped him. His brother Jack worked in a garage in town in his spare time, and helped Billy find just what he needed. It was the first of August when he finally brought it to Marie-Ange, as he came chugging down the driveway in an old Chevy. It sounded terrible, but it drove well, and he had even painted it himself. It was bright red, and the interior was black leather.

He drove up in front of the house, and looked cautiously at Carole when he got out, it was only the third time in seven years that he had been there, and he had never forgotten the reception he'd gotten the first time.

'Wow! Where did you get the fancy car?' Marie-Ange asked with a broad grin, wiping her hands on a towel as she came out of the kitchen. 'Whose is it?'

'I put it together myself. I started right after graduation. Want to drive it?'

She had learned to drive tractors and farm vehicles years before, and often drove her aunt's pickup truck to town to do errands for her or chauffeur her, and she slipped behind the wheel with a broad grin. It was a fun-looking car, although it was old, and Billy had put it together with spit and baling wire, as he said proudly. She drove off the farm, and cruised down the highway for a while, with Billy next to her, and then she reluctantly turned back. She had to cook her aunt's dinner.

'What are you going to do with it? Drive it to church on Sundays?' she asked, smiling at him. She didn't know it, but despite her coloring, she had begun to look just like her mother.

'Nope. I've got better uses for it than that,' he

said mysteriously, proud of himself, and filled with the love for her she would never allow him, except as her adopted brother.

'Like what?' she asked, curious and amused, as they pulled into her driveway.

'It's a school bus.'

'A school bus? What does that mean?'

'It means you get your scholarship. All you need now is money for books. You can drive to school in it every day, Marie-Ange.' He had done it entirely for her, and tears filled her eyes as she looked at him in amazement, and he longed to kiss her, but knew she would never let him.

'You're going to lend it to me?' she asked, lapsing into French. She couldn't believe it, but he shook his head in answer.

'I'm not lending you anything, Marie-Ange. It's a present. It's all yours. Your school bus.'

'Oh, my God! You can't do that!' She threw her arms around his neck and hugged him fiercely. 'Are you serious?' she asked, as she pulled away to look at him. It was the most extraordinary thing anyone had ever done for her, and she hardly knew what to say to him. He had made her dreams come true, and was literally giving her the gift of college, by giving her a way to get there.

'I can do it, and I did. It's all yours, baby.' He was grinning from ear to ear, and she wiped the tears from her cheeks as she watched him. 'Now how about giving me a ride home before your aunt comes out with her shotgun again and shoots me?' They both laughed at the ugly memory, and she went inside to tell her aunt she'd be back in a few minutes. She didn't explain about the car, she was going to do that later.

Billy drove on the way back to his farm, and Marie-Ange sat close to him, exclaiming over how wonderful the car was, how incredible the gift, and how she shouldn't accept it.

'You can't be uneducated forever. You have to get an education so you can get out of here one day.' He knew he never would, he had to help his family keep their farm, and it was always a struggle for them. But he knew his greatest gift to Marie-Ange was her freedom from Aunt Carole.

'I can't believe you'd do this for me,' Marie-Ange said solemnly. She had enormous respect for him, as a person. And she had never been as grateful for anything in her life as she was to him at that moment. And he was happy to see her so ecstatic. She was as excited as he had hoped she would be. He loved everything about her.

She dropped him off and hurried home, and when she told Aunt Carole about what he'd done, at dinner, she forbade her to accept it. 'It's wrong for you to accept a gift like that from him, even if you're planning to marry him,' her aunt said sternly.

'Which I'm not, we're just friends,' Marie-Ange said calmly.

'Then you can't keep it,' Aunt Carole said with a face like wrinkled granite.

But for the first time in seven years of living with her, Marie-Ange was determined to defy her. She would not give up college on the whim of this mean old woman. For seven years she had deprived Marie-Ange in every way she could, of emotion, and food, and love, and money. Theirs had been a life of deprivation in every sense of the word. And now she wanted to rob her of an education, and Marie-Ange would not let her do it.

'I'll borrow it from him then. But I'm going to use it for school,' she said firmly.

'What do you need school for? What do you

think you're going to be? A doctor?' Her tone was derisive.

'I don't know what I'm going to be,' she said quietly. But she knew that it would be more than Aunt Carole. She wanted to be like her mother, although she hadn't gone to university, she had married Marie-Ange's father. But Marie-Ange wanted more than a life on this bleak farm in Iowa, with nothing to enjoy, nothing to celebrate, and nothing to live for. And she knew that one day, when she could escape at last, she would go somewhere, and preferably back to France, at least to visit. But that dream was still on the distant horizon for her. First she had to get an education so she could escape, just as Billy had suggested to her.

'You'll look like a damn fool running around in that old jalopy, particularly if people know who gave it to you.'

'I don't care,' she said defiantly for once, 'I'm proud of it.'

'Then why don't you marry him?' Carole pressed her as she had before, more out of curiosity than real interest. She had never understood the bond between them, and didn't care to.

'Because he is my brother. And I don't want to be married. I want to go home one day,' she said softly.

'This is all the home you have now,' Carole said pointedly, looking Marie-Ange in the eye, and her niece only looked at her, and said nothing. Carole Collins had given her a place to live, a roof over her head, an address, and an endless list of chores to do, but she had never given her kindness, compassion, love, or a sense of family. She had barely celebrated Christmas and Thanksgiving with her. And for all the years Marie-Ange had been there, she had treated her like a servant. Billy and his family had been nicer to her by far than Carole had ever been. And now Billy had given her the one thing she needed to get out of there eventually, and nothing in this world would have made her give that up, and surely not her Aunt Carole.

Marie-Ange cleared away the dishes without saying another word to her, and when her great-aunt went to her room, Marie-Ange picked up the phone and called Billy.

'I just want you to know how much I love you, and how much you mean to me,' she said in French, with a voice filled with emotion, as he wished she meant it in a different sense, but he knew she didn't. He had accepted it for a long time, and he knew that she loved him. 'You are the most wonderful person I know.'

'No, you are,' he said gallantly, but meant it. 'I'm glad you like it, Marie-Ange. I just want you to get out of here, one day. You deserve it.'

'Maybe we'll go together,' she said hopefully, but neither of them believed it. They both knew that Billy was destined to stay, but she wasn't. She still had a long way to go to get out, but thanks to him, she was beginning to believe now that maybe one day she'd make it.

Chapter Five

Marie-Ange started college the week after Labor
Day, and she left the farm at six o'clock, driving
the Chevy that Billy had rebuilt for her. Aunt
Carole made no comment at all the night before,
but as usual, Billy called and wished her good
luck. She promised to stop on the way home, if she
had time, to tell him all about it. But as it turned
out, she left school so late, after buying her books,
with money she had borrowed from Tom, that she
had to rush home to cook dinner for Aunt Carole.

But she managed to stop by to see Billy on her
way to class the next morning. She didn't have to
be at school till ten o'clock, and she dropped by
around seven-thirty, after finishing her chores.
And she spent time with him in the Parkers' big,

friendly kitchen. All their appliances were old, and the Formica counters were chipped. The linoleum floor was stained beyond repair, but his mother kept it immaculately clean, and there was always a warm, cozy atmosphere at their house. Marie-Ange felt at home there, as she had in the kitchen at Marmouton, and unlike her great-aunt, Billy's parents were crazy about her. And Billy's mother believed, because one of her daughters had told her so, that she and Billy would get married someday. But even if they never did, they always treated her like one of their daughters.

'So how was school yesterday?' Billy asked, as he walked into the kitchen with her, in his overalls, and poured them both a cup of coffee.

'It was terrific,' she beamed at him, 'I love it. I wish you were there with me.' The classes he took were at Fort Dodge, and most of the work he did was on his own, and by correspondence.

'So do I,' he smiled back at her. He missed their school days, when he could see her every day, and have long serious talks in French at lunchtime. It was all different now. He had to work on the farm, and he knew that she would have a new life now, new friends, new ideas, professors, and students who had far different goals than he had. He knew he would be on the farm forever. It made him a little sad when he thought about it, but he was happy for her. And after the hard life she'd led on her great-aunt's farm for the past seven years, he knew better than anyone how much it meant to her.

And finally, an hour after she arrived, she got up and had to leave for school, but she promised to come by the following morning.

They saw a lot of each other during her college days, far more than either of them had expected. The commute ate up her time, and she eventually got a job in town as a waitress in a local diner on the weekends, which helped her with expenses, and allowed her to repay the book money she'd borrowed from the foreman. Her Aunt Carole had always refused to give her any money, and told her that if she wanted it badly enough, she'd work for it. But in spite of that, and the chores she still had to do on the farm, she managed to stop and see Billy daily. He came to the diner for a meal occasionally, and now and then they even went to a movie.

During her sophomore year, Billy had a

girlfriend, but he always made it clear to Marie-Ange that she was far more important to him than any other girl and always would be. Their childhood friendship had blossomed into a bond like no other, and she even liked his girlfriend, but by Christmas that year, Billy had tired of her. She didn't have the spark or fire of Marie-Ange, the energy, the brains, the style, and bored him in comparison. Marie-Ange had spoiled him. He turned twenty-one as Marie-Ange started her junior year, and it was a hard year for her. Aunt Carole was sick much of the time, she seemed to be getting old and frail and slowly failing. She was seventy-nine years old by then, and in many ways, she seemed as tough as ever, but it was more bravado than real these days, and from time to time Marie-Ange felt sorry for her, although Billy said he didn't. He had always hated the way she treated Marie-Ange, her hard heart, and mean spirit. Marie-Ange knew by then that her father had not been wrong in his assessment of her. But she was used to her, and grateful to her for taking her in, and she did her best to help her while she was sick. She would prepare food for her late at night, and leave it in the morning, so she would have something to eat all day, and she was far more generous with her portions than Carole had been with her throughout her childhood.

Carole wound up in the hospital at Christmas with a broken hip that year. She had fallen out of her wheelchair when she hit an icy patch on her way to the barn, and for the first time, Marie-Ange spent the entire holiday with Billy. It was the happiest Christmas she'd had in years, and she and his siblings had a grand time, decorating the tree, and making presents for each other, and singing. She brought Aunt Carole a turkey dinner in the hospital, and it saddened her to see that her great-aunt felt too ill to eat it. Her polio didn't make her recovery any easier, and she seemed frailer than ever.

Marie-Ange spent New Year's Eve with Billy too, and she and his brothers and sisters laughed and danced and sang and teased each other until long after midnight. One of his sisters got a little drunk on white wine and asked Marie-Ange when she was finally going to marry Billy. She said that Marie-Ange had ruined him for everyone else anyway, and what was he going to do with all that French he'd learned? Unless he married her, it was useless. And something about the way she said it, though all in good fun and well meant, made Marie-Ange feel guilty.

'Don't be silly,' Billy said, later that night, when she said something to him about it. They were both sober, and sitting on the porch, talking, after everyone else had gone to bed. It was freezing, but they were wrapped up and warm, as they looked up at a starry sky and chatted. 'My sister doesn't know what she's talking about. You haven't "ruined" me, Marie-Ange, you've helped me. Besides, our cows love it when I speak French to them. I was going to write a paper about it for school, I swear they produce more milk if I speak French to them when I milk them.' He was smiling at her, and teasing, and they were holding hands as they did sometimes. There was always something warm and comforting about it, although they both insisted it meant nothing.

'You have to marry someone eventually,' Marie-Ange said practically, but there was a tinge of sadness in her voice as she said it. They both knew that one day their lives would move on, but neither of them was ready for that yet.

'Maybe I'll never marry,' Billy said simply. 'I'm

not sure I want to.' She knew he wanted to marry her, they both knew that, but if he couldn't, he wasn't willing to settle for less than he shared with her. Their friendship was too honest and too deep to make either of them want to settle for less from other partners. And Marie-Ange wanted no one at all at the moment. She liked the life she led, going to school, and sharing all her thoughts and dreams and secrets with Billy. But she was still determined never to confuse or spoil their friendship with romance.

'Don't you want to have children?' Marie-Ange asked, surprised by what he'd said, although she understood the reason for it.

'Maybe. Maybe not. I don't know. I'm going to have a lot of nieces and nephews. They'll drive me crazy enough, maybe I don't need kids of my own.' He looked at her quietly as he said it. All he really wanted was to be with her, and he didn't like the thought of anyone interfering with that. 'You'll have kids one day. I'm sure of that. You'll be a wonderful mother.'

'I can't even imagine it,' she said honestly. She could barely even remember what it was like living in a real family, as she had when her parents and brother were alive. Her only taste of it was when she visited Billy. She loved being there with him, and sharing the love and laughter in his family, but it was no longer part of her life now. In many ways, she felt like a very solitary person.

They talked late into the night, and she spent the night at his house, sharing a bedroom with two of his sisters. And she went back to visit her aunt at the hospital again the next morning. Her recovery was long and slow. And it was nearly a month before she left the hospital, and another two months before she left her bedroom. She didn't seem quite as daunting anymore. Her frailty was growing more visible, and even her meanness seemed to have less force behind it. In a way, she seemed to be shrinking. Marie-Ange did what she had to for her, but the two rarely spoke, and the things Marie-Ange did were more mechanical than driven by any feeling for her.

Carole turned eighty at the beginning of summer, shortly before Marie-Ange turned twenty-one, and it was a major blow to her when her foreman Tom announced that he was retiring and moving to Arizona to be near his wife's parents. His wife had been commuting to see them and care for them all year, and it had just gotten too hard for her.

'Old people like that should be put in a home,' Carole growled at Marie-Ange after Tom had broken the news to her. She was obviously upset, although she had hardly said anything to him, and told Marie-Ange that foremen were a dime a dozen. He had recommended his nephew to her for the job, but Marie-Ange knew that Carole didn't like him. And Marie-Ange was sorry to see Tom go. He had always been kind to her, and she liked him.

Marie-Ange worked full time again that summer to make money to pay for her expenses at school, and she nonetheless managed to spend a fair amount of time with Billy, who had yet another new girlfriend. And this time, Marie-Ange thought it might turn serious if he let it. She was sweet and devoted to him, and very pretty. She had been one grade earlier than they in school, and their families had known each other for years. They could have a very nice life together. And at twenty-two, Marie-Ange thought he was ready. He had been out of high school for three years, finished his extension classes the year before, and worked hard on his father's farm. And like many boys who had worked on farms since his early teens, with all its responsibilities and hardships, he had matured early.

It was a sweltering hot day, and Marie-Ange was just pulling out of the driveway in her beloved Chevy to visit him, when she saw a strange car arrive, driven by an older man in a cowboy hat and a business suit, and she wondered if he was a candidate for the job of foreman. She didn't think about it much, and was surprised to find him still there when she returned from Billy's farm three hours later. It never dawned on her that the man had come to see her, but he was just coming out of the kitchen with her great-aunt, when she got out of the car, with some groceries she had bought to make their dinner. And he looked at her expectantly, as Aunt Carole nodded at her.

Carole introduced the man to her, but his name meant nothing to Marie-Ange. It was Andrew McDermott, and he had driven all the way from Des Moines to see them. He smiled when Marie-Ange asked innocently if he had come to talk to Carole about becoming foreman.

'No, I came to see you,' he said pleasantly. 'I

had some business to discuss with your aunt. Perhaps we could sit down for a little while,' but Marie-Ange knew she had to get dinner on the table, and wondered why he wanted to sit down with her.

'Is something wrong?' Marie-Ange asked her aunt, and the old woman frowned and shook her head. She disapproved of almost everything the man had said, but what he had told her hadn't surprised her. She had known most of it from the beginning.

'No, nothing's wrong,' the visitor said pleasantly. 'I've come to see you about a trust your father left you. Your aunt and I spoke of it some time ago, and the trust's investments have done well over the years. But now that you have reached your majority, I need to inform you of it.' She had no idea what he was talking about, and she could see that Aunt Carole looked anything but pleased. She wondered if her father had done something wrong, or cost her some money. She had no understanding of what he was saying. And she thought that trust was something that happened between two people, like her and Billy. 'Can we sit down while I explain it to you?' They were still standing on the porch, and Marie-Ange left them for a minute to set the groceries down on the kitchen table.

'I won't be long,' she promised Aunt Carole, as the wheelchair disappeared into the house. She had already heard it, and had no interest in staying with them.

'Miss Hawkins,' Andy McDermott began, 'has your aunt explained everything to you about what your father left you?'

Marie-Ange shook her head, looking puzzled. 'No, I didn't think he had left anything. I always thought he had left debts,' she said simply, without artifice or pretension.

'On the contrary,' he looked surprised that she knew nothing about it, 'he left an extremely successful business that was sold some months after he died. One of his partners bought him out, at a fair price, and all the real estate he had was unencumbered. He had some savings, and of course a few debts, but nothing of any magnitude. He left a will, in favor of you and your brother, but on your brother's death, his share passed to you.' It was the first she had heard of any of it, and she was surprised by what he was saying to her. 'You are to inherit a third of what your father left when you turn twenty-one, as you just did, which is why I'm here. And the trust will maintain the rest, and disburse the second third to you at twenty-five, and the balance of it when you turn thirty. He left you a very handsome amount,' he said solemnly, as he looked at Marie-Ange, and realized that she was completely unspoiled and was expecting nothing. Perhaps her aunt had been right not to tell her, he wondered.

'How much did he leave?' Marie-Ange asked, feeling embarrassed. 'Is it a lot?' She didn't think so.

'I'd say it is,' he smiled at her. 'It has been invested well over the years, and at present, before any disbursement to you, the trust is holding just over ten million dollars.' There was a long, long silence, as she stared at him, unable to absorb what he had just said, and unwilling to believe him. This was a joke, it had to be, and it wasn't even funny to her.

'What?' was the only word she could muster.

'The trust is holding just over ten million dollars for you,' he repeated. 'A third of that will be put into an account for you next week, and I suggest

Danielle Steel

that you reinvest the bulk of it as soon as you are prepared to. We can in fact handle that for you.' He was the attorney for the bank who handled her trust account, he explained. The holdings had originally been in France, but had eventually been transferred to Iowa at Carole's suggestion. She didn't think that Marie-Ange would ever go back there. 'I should probably tell you as well,' he said confidentially, 'that we have offered your aunt a sum of money for your support periodically, and she very kindly said there was no need for it. She has provided for you herself for the past ten years, without ever taking advantage of the trust your father left you. I thought you'd like to know that.' But even that piece of information was confusing. Aunt Carole had nearly starved her to death, had bought her clothes at the Goodwill, had forced her to do chores for every penny she'd ever given her, and had refused to help her with college. So while she had shouldered the responsibilities herself, without taking advantage of the trust, she had deprived Marie-Ange of everything possible over the years, and would even have denied her an education, if Billy hadn't given her the car she used to attend college.

It was hard to decide now if Aunt Carole had been a monster or a hero, but perhaps she had done what she thought best. But she had in no way warned Marie-Ange of what was coming to her. It came as a complete surprise, and a huge shock, as Andrew McDermott handed her a manila envelope filled with documents and suggested she review them. He needed only one signature to open an account for her, and as he left, he congratulated her on her good fortune, and even then she wasn't sure if that was how she viewed it. She would far rather have had her parents and brother alive, and grown up with them at Marmouton, than have spent the past ten years in Iowa with Aunt Carole, enduring endless loneliness and hardship. No matter how rich she was now, Marie-Ange still couldn't understand what had just happened to her, or what it would mean to her, as she stood and watched him drive away, as she continued to clutch the envelope he had left her.

'When are we having dinner?' Aunt Carole barked at her through the screen door, and she rushed inside, and put the envelope on the counter as she hurried to prepare dinner. And for the entire meal, Aunt Carole said nothing to her, until Marie-Ange broke the silence.

'Did you know?' Her eyes searched her great-aunt's face and saw nothing, not affection or warmth or regret or tenderness or joy for her. She looked as she always had, bitter and tired and old and as cold as ice in winter.

'Not all of it. I still don't. It's none of my business. I know your father left you a lot of money. I'm glad for you. It'll make things easier for you when I'm gone,' and then she stunned Marie-Ange further. 'I'm selling the farm next month. I've had a good offer, and you're all right now. I'm tired. I'm going to move into the home in Boone.' She said it without apology or regret, or any concern about what would happen to Marie-Ange, but admittedly she had no reason to worry about her, except that she was a girl of twenty-one, and for the second time in her life, she was about to become homeless.

'How much longer will you stay here?' Marie-Ange asked, looking concerned about her, and seeking some trace of emotion that had never been there.

'If I sell next month, it'll be in escrow for thirty

days. I should be in the home by the end of October. Tom said he would wait till then.' But it was only six weeks away, and Marie-Ange realized that she was going to have to make some decisions. She was about to start her senior year, and wondered if she should move closer to school, or take the year off to go home to France and at least see it. And for an instant, she had a brief dream about buying Marmouton back. She had no idea who owned it now, or what had happened to it, and wondered if that information would be included in the papers the lawyer from the bank had left her.

'I'll have to move out when you do,' Marie-Ange said pensively, wondering if she had ever known this woman. But she already knew the answer to that question. 'Will you be happy in the home, Aunt Carole?' She felt as though she owed her something, however disagreeable she had been, or cold. She had still taken care of her for ten years, and Marie-Ange was grateful for it.

'I'm not happy here. What difference does it make? And I'm too old to run a farm now. You'll go back to France, I expect, or get a job somewhere, after you finish college. You have no reason to stay here, unless you marry that boy you say you don't want to marry. And you probably shouldn't now. You can catch yourself a real big fish with all that money.' She made it sound like an ugly thing, and the way she said it made Marie-Ange shudder. The idea of loving someone never entered into it for her, and Marie-Ange couldn't help wondering, as she had before, what her life had been like with her husband, and if she had ever loved him, if she was even capable of it. It was impossible to imagine her young or loving or happy.

Marie-Ange cleaned up the kitchen after their meal, and her aunt said she was going to bed early, and wheeled herself silently down the dark hallway. But when Billy called a short time afterward, Marie-Ange said she had to see him.

'Is something wrong?' He sounded worried.

'No . . . yes . . . no . . . I don't know. I'm confused. Something happened today I have to talk to you about.' She needed to talk to him very badly. There was no one else for her to talk to, although she knew he was as unsophisticated as she was about financial matters. But he was sensible and intelligent, and he wanted nothing but the best for her. It never occurred to her for an instant that he'd be jealous of her.

'Are you okay?' he asked, and she hesitated.

'I think so. Yes.' She didn't want to worry him. 'It's a good thing. I just don't understand it.'

'Come over whenever you want,' he said comfortably. His new girlfriend was there, but she lived on a nearby farm, and he offered to run her home before Marie-Ange came over, and she didn't seem to mind it.

Marie-Ange was on his front porch twenty minutes later, and she had brought the manila envelope with her. 'What's that?' He noticed it instantly, and wondered if it was a transcript from college. He wondered suddenly if she had won another scholarship, but the look on her face told him it was something more important.

'A lawyer came to see me today,' she said in an undervoice, so the rest of the family couldn't hear what she was saying to him, and she trusted him completely. Her faith in him had never been unfounded, and she knew it wouldn't be this time.

'What about?'

'Some money my father left me when he died,' she said simply, and his mind went swiftly, as hers had, to amounts in the thousands, if she was lucky. At least it would help her finish her education, and he was happy for her. 'A lot of money,' she tried to adjust his thinking for him. But what had happened to her was inconceivable, and she knew Billy wouldn't understand it any better than she did.

'Like how much?' And then he corrected himself quickly, 'Or would you rather not tell me? You don't have to, you know. It's none of my business,' he said discreetly.

'I guess I shouldn't say anything,' she said, looking at him, terrified that it would change something between them. 'I don't want you to hate me for it.'

'Don't be stupid. Did he kill someone for it, or steal it?' he teased her.

'Of course not,' she smiled nervously at him, 'it's from the house and his business, and some investments. What he left has grown a lot in the last ten years. Billy,' she hesitated for a long moment, 'it's a *lot* of money.' She suddenly wanted to apologize for it. It seemed sinful to have that much. But she did. And now she had to deal with it.

'You're driving me crazy, Marie-Ange. Are you going to tell me or not? And did your Aunt Carole know, by the way?' He was curious about it.

'Apparently, she did, more or less. And she never let them give her anything to support me. I guess that's nice in a way, but it sure would have made life easier if she had. Anyway, it's all mine now.' Their eyes met and held as he waited, and she took a breath and whispered the words to him that even she didn't understand, and wondered if she ever would. It was beyond thinking. 'Ten million dollars,' she said, barely loud enough for him to hear her.

'Yeah, sure,' he said, laughing at her, and sitting back in his chair on the porch, amused by the joke. He had been leaning forward waiting to hear, and now he just guffawed at her. 'And I'm Mickey Mantle.'

'No, I'm serious. That's what it is.' She looked as though she was sharing something terrible with him, and suddenly he stopped laughing and stared at her.

'You're not kidding?' She shook her head in answer, and he closed his eyes as though she had hit him, and then opened them to look at her in disbelief. 'Oh, my God, Marie-Ange . . . what are you going to do with it? What are you going to do now?' In a way, it scared him for her. It was an overwhelming amount of money. Beyond either of their imaginations.

'I don't know. Aunt Carole told me tonight she's selling the farm next month and going into the home in Boone. I'm not going to have anyplace to live six weeks from now. She already has someone who wants to buy the farm, and she's decided to sell it to them.'

'You can live here,' he said generously, but she knew there was no room for her, and she knew that wasn't right either.

'I could get an apartment at school, I guess, or live in the dorm. I don't know what you do when something like this happens.'

'Neither do I,' he grinned shyly at her. 'Your father must have been one hell of a rich guy when you were a kid. I guess I never understood that. That château you talk about must have been the size of Buckingham Palace.'

'No, it wasn't. It was beautiful, and I loved it, I guess there was a lot of land, and his business must have been pretty successful. He had money saved too, and . . . God, Billy, I don't know . . . what'll I do now?' She had come to him for advice, but they were both young, and what they were talking about was inconceivable to either of them, particularly given the life they both led. Their lives in Iowa were very simple.

'What do you want to do?' he asked her thoughtfully. 'Do you want to go home, and start over there, or finish school here? You can do anything you want now. Hell, Marie-Ange, you can go to Harvard if you want to.' To him, at least, it represented an unlimited amount of freedom, and he was happy for her.

'I think I'd like to go home for a while, and at least see Marmouton again. Maybe I could even buy it.' And never come back here, he could hear the reality of it echo in his head as he listened to her, but he didn't voice his fears to her. He was suddenly afraid he'd never see her again when she left. But she knew what he was thinking.

'I'll come back. I just want to see what it looks like. Maybe I'll take a semester off, and come back here for Christmas.'

'That would be nice,' and then he decided to put his own feelings aside and think of her. He loved her enough to do that. 'But you might be happier there.' She was French, after all, and she had no relatives in the States except Aunt Carole. And although she had spent nearly half her life here, in her heart of hearts, she was still French, and always would be.

'Maybe. I just don't know what to do now.' She didn't feel as though either place was home anymore. And with options open to her, it was all the more confusing. 'If I stayed, would you come to visit me? You could use your French finally. I'd send you a ticket.' She knew him well enough to know he would never accept it, and it would be a hardship for him to take the time to visit her even if he had the money to buy the ticket. 'You have to promise me you'd come over if I stay there.'

'Do you think you'll finish school?' he asked, concerned about her again, and she nodded.

'I want to. I think I probably will come back here. Maybe I'll just take this semester off and see what happens.'

'It would be a shame not to finish school,' he said, sounding like an older brother, as she nodded.

She took the contents of the envelope out then,

and they pored over them together. But neither of them understood them. It was the portfolio of the trust's investments.

'I just can't believe it,' he said, looking at her again before she left. 'Marie-Ange, this is amazing,' and then he grinned at her and gave her a hug. 'Hell, who knew you'd turn out to be a rich girl.'

'I feel like Cinderella,' she whispered.

'Just make sure you don't run off with a handsome prince in the next ten minutes.' He knew this meant that there was no hope for them, but according to Marie-Ange, there never had been. And now there was no way he could ever ask her. She was an heiress, but she was also his best friend, and she made him swear it would never make any difference between them.

'I'll be back for Christmas,' she promised faithfully, and meant it as she said it. But he wondered if that would be true, if she really would come back, or even want to, after the miserable years she'd spent here. It seemed right to him that she should go home now.

He walked her out to the car when she left, and gave her another hug. The car he had given her seemed foolish to him now in light of everything that had just happened. 'Drive carefully,' he smiled at her, still in awe of what she had told him. They both needed time to absorb it.

'I love you, Billy,' she said, and meant it in the very best of ways, and he knew that.

'I love you too. You know that.' And with that, she waved and drove away. She had a lot to think about on the drive home, and she drove to Des Moines the next morning. There was something she knew she had to do there. She had thought of it the night before, and she didn't want to wait another day. She called Andy McDermott and explained it to him, and he sounded a little startled at first, but she was only twenty-one, after all. It was an interesting first step, but she was very determined when he questioned her about it.

She completed the transaction in under an hour, and they agreed to deliver it to the farm for her that morning. They were stunned by the speed with which she had made the purchase. And when it arrived, it caused endless comment amongst the farmhands, and Aunt Carole was livid when she saw it.

'That is just the kind of stupid thing I thought

you would do. What are you going to do with that thing?' she asked accusingly, but there was nothing she could do to stop her.

'I'm giving it to Billy,' Marie-Ange said calmly, as she slid behind the wheel of the bright red, brand-new Porsche she had bought for him that morning. Three years before he had made it possible for her to go to school and get an education, and now she was going to do something for him, something he could never do for himself in a lifetime. She had paid the insurance on it for him for two years, and she knew he was going to love it.

She drove it up in front of his house, just as he came in on the tractor with one of his brothers, and he stared at her in amazement.

'Did you trade the Chevy in for that? I hope they gave you back some money!' He laughed and hopped off the tractor to look more closely at the remarkable machine she was driving. 'How are you going to tell people you bought it?' he asked, looking concerned. He knew she didn't want everyone talking about her, or knowing what she'd inherited from her father.

'I haven't figured that out yet,' she grinned at

him, 'maybe I'll just have to tell them I stole it. But at least I won't be driving it.'

'Why not?' He looked confused, as she quietly handed him the keys and kissed him on both cheeks, French style.

'Because it's yours, Billy!' she said softly. 'Because you're the best friend I have in the world, and you're my brother.'

Tears welled up in his eyes, and he didn't know what to say to her, and when he could finally speak again, he insisted that he couldn't accept it from her, no matter how much money her father had left her. But she refused to discuss it with him, or to be swayed. The pink slip was already in his name, and she slid into the passenger seat, waiting for him to drive her in it.

'I don't know what to say to you,' he said in a choked voice as he slid behind the wheel. It was hard to resist, and everyone on his father's farm was staring at them. They knew something unbelievable had just happened.

'Does this mean you're marrying him?' his mother shouted from the kitchen window, wondering if she had won it in a contest for him. Maybe she had won the lottery or something.

'No, it means he has a new car,' Marie-Ange shouted back at her with a grin, as Billy turned the key in the ignition and the little sports car roared into gear. They took off at full speed, as Billy gave a wild whoop of glee, and Marie-Ange's long blond hair flew out in the wind behind her.

Chapter Six

Aunt Carole sold the farm, just as she had said she would, and two weeks later she moved to the home in Boone. Marie-Ange helped her pack her things, and she couldn't help thinking of Carole's cruelty when she had taken Marie-Ange's suitcases to the Goodwill and left them there with nearly everything she'd brought with her. But this time, Marie-Ange packed all her little mementos and favorite belongings for her. And when they reached the home, the old woman turned to her, and looked at her long and hard, and said, 'Don't do anything stupid.'

'I'll try not to,' Marie-Ange smiled, wanting to feel more for her than she did, but she just didn't. Aunt Carole had never allowed it. Marie-Ange couldn't even tell her that she'd miss her. They both knew she wouldn't. 'I'll write to you, and tell you where I am,' she said politely.

'You don't have to. I don't like to write. I can call the bank, if I need to find you.' After ten years of living together, it was a dry, unemotional departure. Carole was simply not capable of more than that, and never had been. And after Marie-Ange left her, she felt sad, for all that had never happened between them. Emotionally at least, except for Billy, it had been ten years wasted.

She went back to the house and packed her things. Tom and his wife were already gone, and the house seemed strange and empty. Marie-Ange had her ticket and her passport, and her bags were packed. She was leaving in the morning, back the way she had come, first to Chicago, and then to Paris. She was going to stay there for a few days, and maybe look into classes at the Sorbonne, and then she was going to rent a car and drive to Marmouton, just to see it. And she was going to find out what had happened to Sophie. She assumed that she had died, but maybe someone could tell her how or when it had happened. Marie-Ange suspected she had died of a broken heart, but whatever had happened to her, she wanted to know it. She knew that if Sophie had been alive, she'd have written to her, and she hadn't. Not a single letter in answer to her own, or since then.

She ate dinner with Billy and his family that night. Everyone in the area was still talking about his new Porsche, and he drove it every chance he got. His father had teased him that he spent more time in it than on the tractor. And his girlfriend Debbi was in love with it. But it meant the most to Billy because Marie-Ange had given it to him. He had finally stopped arguing with her about it, and agreed to accept it, although he said he shouldn't have, but he couldn't bring himself to part with it. It was his dream car, and her thank-you for getting her to college in the Chevy.

'I'll call you from Paris, when I can,' she promised him that night when he took her home. She had left the Chevy with him, and asked him to store it for her, in case she came back to finish college. She didn't want to sell it, it meant too much to her. It was the only thing she wanted to keep from her years with Aunt Carole. There were no other happy memories for her, only sad ones, except those that involved Billy.

Billy promised to pick her up in the morning and drive her to the airport. And as she wandered the house alone, thinking of the ten years she had spent there, it seemed eerie and agonizingly lonely. She wondered how her great-aunt was at the home, but Carole had told her not to bother calling, so she didn't.

She slept fitfully that night, and did no chores when she got up, for the first time in more than ten years. And it was strangest of all to realize that soon she would be in Paris, and then back at Marmouton. She couldn't even imagine what she would find there.

Billy picked her up promptly at nine, and put her one small bag in the car. She had almost nothing to take with her. She had no souvenirs, no photographs, except of him, no mementos, except the things he had made her over the years, for her birthdays and at Christmas. The only other things that meant anything to her were the photographs of her parents and Robert, and the locket she still wore and treasured.

They were both quiet in the car, on the way to the airport. There was so much to say, and no way to say it. They had said it to each other over the years, and been there for each other, as they still were now. But they both knew that with 5,000 miles between them, it couldn't help but be different.

'Call me if you need me,' he said, as they waited for her plane to Chicago to board. She hadn't been on a plane since she had come here, and she remembered how terrified she had been, how heartbroken, and how lonely. He had been her only friend for all these years, her only source of strength and comfort. Her great-aunt had provided room and board, but there had never been any love between them. Billy was her family far more than Aunt Carole had ever been, and as she boarded the plane finally, Marie-Ange held him tight for a long moment as tears streamed down both their faces.

'I'm going to miss you so much,' she cried. It was like leaving Robert again, and she was afraid now that she would never see Billy again, just as she had lost her brother. But he sensed her thoughts without her needing to put words to them, and he quietly reassured her.

'It'll be okay. You'll probably hate France and

be back here in no time.' But he didn't believe that.

'Take care of yourself,' she said softly to him, and they kissed and hugged for a last time, and she looked up at him, wanting to engrave his freckled face on her mind forever. 'I love you, Billy.'

'I love you too, Marie-Ange,' he said, wishing she could stay in Iowa forever. But it wouldn't have been fair to her, and he knew that. She had a chance for so much more now.

He stood and waved at the plane until it was a speck in the sky, and then she was gone. And he drove slowly back to the farm in his new red car, crying for all that she had been to him, and never would be.

Chapter Seven

The plane touched down at Charles de Gaulle at four A.M., and with her single bag, it only took Marie-Ange a few minutes to go through customs. And it felt strange suddenly to hear people speaking French everywhere, and it made her smile as she thought of Billy and how well he had learned it.

She took a cab to a small hotel one of the stewardesses had recommended to her. It was on the Left Bank, and it was safe and clean, and after she had washed her face, and unpacked her bag, it was time for breakfast. She decided to walk around outside and found a little café where she ordered croissants and coffee. And just for the sheer joy of it, she made herself a *canard* in the cup of steaming café au lait, and thought of Robert. It brought back so many memories, she could hardly bear it. Afterward, she walked for hours, looking at people, enjoying the scene, relishing the feeling of being in France again. She didn't go back to her hotel for hours, and when she did, she was exhausted.

She had dinner in a little bistro, and cried in her bed in the hotel that night, for her brother and her parents, and the years she had lost, and then she cried for the friend she had left in Iowa. But in spite of her sadness, she loved being in Paris. She went to the Sorbonne the next day, and took some brochures with her about the classes they offered. And the following morning, she rented a car, and made her way to Marmouton. It took her all day to get there. And she could feel her heart pound, as she drove slowly through the village, and on a whim, she stopped at the bakery she had loved as a child, and stared in disbelief when she saw the same old woman behind the counter. She had been a close friend of Sophie's.

Marie-Ange spoke to her cautiously, and explained who she was, and the old woman began to cry the moment she recognized her.

'My God, you are so beautiful, and so grown-up! Sophie would have been so proud of you,' she said as she embraced her.

'What happened to her?' Marie-Ange asked as the woman handed her a brioche across the counter.

'She died last year,' the woman at the bakery said sadly.

'I wrote to her so often, and she never answered. Was she ill for a long time?' Perhaps she'd had a stroke, Marie-Ange thought, as soon as she'd left her. It was the only possible explanation for her silence.

'No, she went to live with her daughter when you left, and she came to visit me every few years. We always talked about you. She said she wrote to you nearly a hundred times the first year, and all her letters came back unopened. She gave up after that, she thought maybe she had the wrong address, but your father's lawyer told her it was the right one. Perhaps someone didn't want you to see her letters.' Marie-Ange felt her words like a blow to her heart, as she realized that Aunt Carole must have returned Sophie's letters to her, and thrown Marie-Ange's letters away, to sever her ties with her past. It was just the kind of thing Carole would do. It was yet another act of cruelty, but so needless and so unkind, and now Sophie was gone forever. She felt her loss now as though it had just happened. 'I'm sorry,' the woman added, seeing the young girl's face, and the pain etched on it.

'Who lives at the château now?' Marie-Ange asked quietly. It was not easy coming back here, it was full of bittersweet memories for her, and she knew it would break her heart when she saw the château again, but she felt she had to, to pay homage to the past, to touch a part of her family again, as though if she returned, she would find them, but of course she knew she wouldn't.

'A count owns it. The Comte de Beauchamp. He lives in Paris, and no one ever sees him. He rarely comes here. But you can take a look if you want. The gates are always open. He has a caretaker, perhaps you remember him. Madame Fournier's grandson.' Marie-Ange remembered him well from the farm at Marmouton, he was only a few years older than she was, and they had played together once in a while as children. He had helped her climb a tree once, and Sophie had scolded them both and forced them to come down. She wondered if he remembered it as clearly as she did.

She thanked the woman at the bakery and left, promising to return, and she drove slowly the rest of the way to the château, and when she reached it, she found, as the woman had said, that the gates were open, which surprised her, particularly if the owner was more often than not absent.

Marie-Ange parked her rented car outside the grounds, and walked slowly through the gates, as though she were reentering Paradise and was afraid that someone would stop her. But no one came, there was no sound, no sign of life. And Alain Fournier was nowhere in sight. The château looked abandoned. The shutters were closed, the grounds were somewhat overgrown, there was a sad look to the place now, and she could see that part of the roof was in disrepair. And beyond the house, she saw the familiar fields and trees, woods and orchards. It was precisely as she had remembered. It was as though, just seeing it, she was a child again, and Sophie would come looking for her at any moment. Her brother would still be there, and her parents would come home from their activities in time for dinner. And as she stood very still, she could hear birds, and wished that she could climb a tree again. The air was cool, and the place, even in its disrepair, was more beautiful than ever. For a moment, she wished that Billy could see it. It was exactly as she had described it to him.

She walked out into the fields, with her head bowed, thinking of the family she'd lost, the years she'd been away, the life she had loved so much and that had ended so abruptly. And now she was back, and it belonged to someone else. It made her heart ache to know that. She sat on a rock in the fields, reliving a thousand tender memories, and then as night fell slowly in the cool October air, she began to walk back slowly toward the courtyard. She had just passed the kitchen door, when a sports car pulled in at full speed, and stopped near her. The man behind the wheel looked at her with a puzzled expression, and then smiled at her and got out. He was tall and thin, with dark hair and green eyes, and he looked very aristocratic. She wondered instantly if he was the Comte de Beauchamp.

'Are you lost? Do you need help?' he asked pleasantly, and she noticed the gold crest ring on his finger, indicating that he was noble.

'No, I'm sorry. I'm trespassing,' she said, thinking of how her great-aunt had fired her shotgun the first time Billy came to visit. But this man's manners were a great deal better than her Aunt Carole's.

'It's a pretty place, isn't it?' he said with a smile. 'I wish I spent more time here.'

'It's beautiful,' she said with a sad smile, as another car came through the gate and stopped near them, and as a young man got out, she saw that it was his caretaker, Alain Fournier. 'Alain?' she said, before she could stop herself. He was short and powerful and had the same pleasant face he had had as a child when they played together. And he recognized her immediately, although her hair was long and no longer in curls, but it was the same golden color it always had been. And although she had grown up, she hadn't changed much.

'Marie-Ange?' he said with a look of amazement.

'Are you friends?' the count said with a look of amusement.

'We were,' the caretaker answered as he held out a hand to shake Marie-Ange's, 'we played

together as children. When did you come back?'
he asked her with a look of wonder.

'Just now ... today ...' She looked apologetically at the new owner of the château. 'I'm
sorry. I just wanted to see it.'

'Did you live here?' the count asked, puzzled by
this brief exchange.

'Yes. As a child. My parents ... I ... they died
a long time ago, and I went to America to live with
my great-aunt. I just drove down from Paris
today.'

'So did I,' he smiled benignly at her, looking
polite and well bred and pleasant as Alain waved
at her and slipped away. The count was wearing a
blue blazer and gray flannels, and his clothes
looked impeccably cut and expensive. 'Would you
like to come inside and look around?' She
hesitated for a long moment, not wanting to
intrude further on him, but the offer was
irresistible. And he could see in her eyes that she
would love to. 'I insist that you come inside. It's
getting cold out here. I'll make a pot of tea, and
you can wander.' Without a word, she followed
him gratefully into the familiar kitchen. And as
she did, she felt her lost world envelop her, and

tears stung her eyes as she looked around her. 'Has it changed much?' he asked her gently, unaware of the circumstances of her parents' accident, but it was easy to see that this was an emotional moment for her. 'Why don't you walk around for a while, and when you come back, I'll have your tea ready.' It was embarrassing to have barged in on him in this way, but he was so nice about it.

'It has hardly changed at all,' she said, with a look of tender amazement. In fact, the same table and chairs were there, where she had had breakfast and lunch every day with her parents and Robert. It was the same table Robert had passed the sugary *canards* under as they dripped coffee on the carpet. 'Did you buy the château from my father's estate?' she asked, as he took out the teapot and an antique silver strainer.

'No. I bought it from a man who had owned it for several years but never lived here. I think his wife was ill, or she didn't like it. He sold it to me, and I have been planning to spend some time here and restore it. I haven't owned it for long, and I've been too busy to pay much attention to it. But I'm hoping to get to work on it this winter, or at least next spring. It deserves to be as beautiful as it once was.' It looked undeniably tired and untended.

'It doesn't look as though it would take much work to do it,' Marie-Ange said to her host as he poured the tea through the strainer. The walls needed some paint, and the floors needed wax, but to her, it still looked wonderful and so precisely as she remembered. But he smiled at her assessment.

'I'm afraid the plumbing is in sad shape, and the electrical wires have all gone wrong. It needs a great deal of work you can't even see. Believe me, it's a big undertaking. And both the vineyards and the orchards need to be replanted . . . it needs a new roof. I'm afraid, Mademoiselle, that I have let your family home fall into sad disrepair,' he said apologetically with a smile that was filled with charm and wit and spirit. 'By the way, I'm Bernard de Beauchamp.' He extended a hand to her, and they shook hands politely.

'Marie-Ange Hawkins.' As she said it, something clicked in his memory, and he remembered a story about a terrible accident that had claimed three lives and left a little girl an orphan. The man he'd bought it from had bought the château from her father's estate, and told Bernard the story.

Danielle Steel

He shooed her off to the living room then, and heard her go upstairs to visit her old bedroom. And when she came back downstairs, he could see that she'd been crying and felt sorry for her.

'It must be hard for you to come back here,' he said, handing her the cup of tea he'd made for her. It was strong and dark and pungent and helped to restore her, as he invited her to sit at the familiar kitchen table.

'It's harder than I thought,' she admitted to him, as she sat down, looking very young and very pretty. He was almost exactly twice her age. He had just turned forty.

'That's to be expected,' he said solemnly. 'I remember hearing about your parents, and about you,' he smiled at her, and there was nothing wicked or lascivious about him. He just looked like a nice man, and seemed like a sympathetic person. 'I've had my own taste of that. I lost my wife and son ten years ago in a fire, in a house like this. I sold the château, and it took me a long time to get over it, if one ever does. That's why I wanted to buy this one, because I longed to have a house like this again, but it has been hard for me. Perhaps that's why it has taken me a while to do it. But it will be lovely when I get around to it.'

'It was lovely when I lived here,' Marie-Ange smiled gratefully at him for his kindness. 'My mother always had it filled with flowers.'

'And what were you like then?' he smiled gently at her.

'I spent all my time climbing trees and picking fruit in the orchards.' They both laughed at the image she painted for him.

'Well, you've certainly grown up since then,' he said, seeming pleased to be sharing a cup of tea with her. It was lonely for him there, for the reasons he had just explained to her, and he enjoyed her company. She had been a pleasant surprise for him when he got there. 'I'm going to be here for a month this time. I want to work on the plans for the remodeling with the local builder. You'll have to come and visit me again, if you have time. Will you be staying here long?' he asked with curiosity, and she looked uncertain.

'I'm not sure yet. I just arrived from the States two days ago, and all I knew I wanted to do was come here. I want to go to Paris, and see about taking classes at the Sorbonne.'

'Have you moved back to France yet?'

'I don't know,' she said honestly, 'I haven't decided. My father left . . .' She caught herself on the words. It would have been indelicate to mention the trust her father had left her. 'I have an opportunity to do what I want now, and I have to make some decisions about it.'

'That's a good spot to be in,' he said, as he refilled her cup of tea and they went on talking. 'Where are you staying, Miss Hawkins?'

'I don't know that yet either,' she said, laughing and realizing she must have sounded very young and foolish to him. He seemed so grown-up and sophisticated. 'And please call me Marie-Ange.'

'I would be delighted to do so.' His manners were impeccable, his charm impossible to ignore, his looks impressive. 'I just had a very strange idea, and perhaps you will think me mad for suggesting it, but perhaps you would like it. If you haven't made any other arrangements yet, I was wondering if you might like to stay here, Marie-Ange. You don't know me at all, but you can lock all the doors in your wing, if you like. I actually sleep in the guest room because I like it better. I find it sunnier and more cheerful. But the entire master suite can be sealed off quite effectively, and you would be safe from me, if you're worried about it. But it might mean something to you to stay here.' She sat and stared at him, overwhelmed by the offer, and unable to believe that things like that happened. And she wasn't in the least afraid of him. He was so well brought up and so polite that she knew she had nothing to fear from him. And all she wanted was to stay here and steep herself in the past and the memories she had missed for half her lifetime.

'It would be incredibly rude of me to stay here, wouldn't it?' she asked him cautiously, afraid to take advantage of his kindness, but dying to stay there.

'Not if I invite you, and I did. I meant it. I wouldn't have offered it if I didn't want you to stay here. I can't imagine you'd be much trouble.' He smiled at her in a fatherly way, and without letting herself think about it further, she accepted, and promised to leave for Paris the next day. 'Stay as long as you like,' he assured her. 'I told you, I'll be here for a month, on holiday, and the place gets rather dreary when I'm alone.' She wanted to offer to pay for her room, but she was afraid to insult him. He was obviously prosperous, and what's more, he was a count. She didn't want to offend him by treating the château like a hotel. 'What shall we do for dinner, by the way? Do you have plans, or should I whip something up? I'm not a great cook, but I can come up with something edible. I have some groceries in my car.'

'I don't expect you to feed me as well.' She looked embarrassed to be that much of a burden on him. She had no sense of how pleased he was to have her around. 'I could cook for you, if you like,' she offered shyly. She had cooked for her Aunt Carole every night. The meals had been plain, but her aunt had never complained about them.

'Do you know how to cook?' He looked amused at the thought.

'In America, I had to cook for my great-aunt.'

'Rather like Cinderella?' he teased as his green eyes danced in amusement.

'A bit like that,' Marie-Ange said, taking her empty cup to the all-too-familiar sink. Even standing there brought back countless memories of Sophie. And once more she thought of Sophie's letters and what she'd learned about them that day.

'I will cook for you,' he promised her. But in the end, they both settled for pâté, the fresh baguette he had bought, and some brie. And he brought out an excellent bottle of red wine, which she declined.

She set the table for him, and they chatted for a long time.

He was from Paris, and had lived in England briefly as a child, and then come back to France. And after they had talked for a while, he said that his little boy had been four years old when he died in the fire. He said he thought he would never recover from it, and he hadn't in some ways. He had never remarried, and admitted that he led a solitary life. But he didn't seem like a morose sort of man, and he made Marie-Ange laugh much of the time.

They left each other at ten o'clock, after he had made sure that there were clean sheets on the bed in the master suite. He made no overtures to her, did nothing inappropriate, wished her a good night, and disappeared to the guest suite on the opposite side of the house.

But it was harder than she thought sleeping in her parents' bed, and thinking about them, and to get there, she had walked past her own room, and Robert's. Her head and heart were full of them all through the night.

Chapter Eight

When Marie-Ange came down for breakfast the next day, after making her bed, she looked tired.

'How did you sleep?' he asked with a look of concern. He was drinking café au lait, and reading the paper Alain had bought him in town.

'Oh . . . I have a lot of memories here, I guess,' she said thoughtfully, thinking that she shouldn't disturb him more than she had, and that she could get breakfast in town.

'I was afraid of that. I thought about it last night,' he said, as he poured her a huge cup of café au lait. 'These things take time.'

'It's been ten years,' she said, sipping the coffee, and thinking of Robert's clandestine *canards*.

'But you've never come back here,' he said

sensibly. 'That is bound to be hard. Would you like to go for a walk in the woods today, or visit the farm?'

'No, you're very kind,' she smiled, 'I should drive back to Paris today.' There was no point staying here anymore. She had had one night to touch her memories, but it was his house now, and time for her to move on.

'Do you have appointments in Paris?' he asked comfortably. 'Or do you simply feel you ought to go?'

She smiled as she nodded, as he silently admired her long blond hair, but she saw nothing frightening in his eyes. The idea that she had spent a night alone in the house with him would have shocked most people, she knew, but it had been so chaste, and so harmless, and so polite.

'I think you ought to have time to enjoy your house, without a stranger camping out in your master suite,' she said with serious eyes as she looked at him. 'You've been very kind, Monsieur le Comte, but I have no right to be here anymore.'

'You have every right to be here, as my guest. In fact, if you have the time, I would love your advice, and the benefit of your memory, to tell me exactly how the house was before. Do you have time for that?' In fact, she had nothing but time on her hands, and she couldn't believe his enormous kindness to her, in inviting her to stay on.

'Are you sure?' she asked him honestly.

'Very sure. And I would much prefer it if you called me Bernard.'

Before lunch, they took a walk in the fields, and she told him precisely how everything had been, as they walked all the way to the farm, and then he called Alain to pick them up, so he didn't wear her out walking back.

She went into town to buy groceries and bought several excellent bottles of wine for him, to thank him for his incredible hospitality. And this time, when she suggested she cook dinner for them, he offered to take her out. That night he took her to a cozy bistro nearby, which hadn't been there ten years before, and they had a very good time. He had a thousand tales to tell, and an easy way of speaking to her, as though they were old friends. He was a very charming, amusing, intelligent man.

They parted company outside her parents' room again, and this time, when she climbed into bed, she fell asleep at once. And the next day, when she got up, she told him a little more strenuously that she thought she should move on.

'I must have done something to offend you then,' he said, pretending to look wounded, and then smiled. 'I told you, I would be so grateful for your help if you'd stay, Marie-Ange.' It was crazy. She had literally moved into the house with him, a complete stranger who had landed on him. And in spite of her embarrassment, which he dispelled easily, he didn't seem to mind.

'But won't you stay through next weekend?' he asked pleasantly. 'I'm giving a dinner party, and I would love to introduce you to some friends. They'd be fascinated by what you know of Marmouton. One of them is the architect who is going to draw up my remodeling plans. I'd appreciate it so much if you'd stay. In fact, I don't know why you're leaving at all. There's no need for you to rush back to Paris. You said yourself you have time.'

'Aren't you tired of me yet?' She looked worried for a minute, and then smiled. He was so convincing about wanting her to hang around, almost as though he'd been expecting her, and didn't mind at all that she had taken over the master suite and invaded his house. He treated her like an expected houseguest and good friend, instead of the intruder she was.

'Why would I be tired of you? What a silly thing to say. You're charming company, and you've helped me immeasurably, explaining to me about the house.' She had even showed him a secret passage that she and Robert had loved, and he was fascinated by it. Even Alain hadn't known about it, and he had grown up at the farm. 'Now, will you stay? If you must go, which I don't believe at all, at least put it off until after the weekend.'

'Are you quite sure you don't want me to go?'

'On the contrary, not at all. I want you to stay, Marie-Ange.'

She continued to buy groceries for him, and he cooked for her. They went back to the same bistro again, and then she cooked for him the next night. And by the time the weekend came, they had become old friends. They bantered easily in the morning over their café au lait, he discussed politics with her, and explained to her what had been going on in France. He told her about the people he knew, the friends he liked best, asked

145

her about her family at length, and now and then reminisced about his late wife and son. He told her he had worked for a bank, and was now doing consulting work, which gave him a remarkable amount of free time. And he had worked so hard for so many years, and been so devastated after he lost his wife and son, that he was finally enjoying taking a break from the rat race for a while. It all sounded very sensible to Marie-Ange.

And by the time she'd been there a week, she decided to call Billy from the post office, just to tell him where she was. She called him from the telephone *cabine*, because she didn't want to make a transatlantic call on Bernard's phone.

'Guess where I am!' she chortled excitedly the moment Billy came to the phone.

'Let me guess. Paris. At the Sorbonne.' He was still hoping she'd come back to finish college in Iowa, and he felt a flicker of disappointment to think that she might have enrolled at the Sorbonne.

'Better than that. Guess again.' She loved teasing him, and had missed talking to him since she'd been gone.

'I give up,' he said easily.

'I'm in Marmouton. Staying at the château.'

146

'Have they turned it into a hotel?' He sounded pleased for her, and he hadn't heard her sound that happy in a long time. She sounded rested and content, and at peace with her memories. He was glad she had gone to Marmouton after all.

'No, it's still a private house. There's a terribly nice man living there, and he let me stay.'

'Does he have a family?' Billy sounded concerned, and she laughed at the tone of his voice.

'He did. He lost his wife and son in a fire.'

'Recently?'

'Ten years ago,' she said confidently. She knew she had nothing to fear from Bernard. He had proven himself ever since she'd arrived, and she trusted him as her friend. But it was hard to explain that to Billy over the phone. It was just something she felt, and she trusted her instincts about the man.

'How old is he?'

'He's forty,' she said, as though he were a hundred years old. And compared to her, he was.

'Marie-Ange, that's dangerous,' Billy scolded her sensibly. 'You're living alone at the château with a forty-year-old widower? What exactly is going on?'

Danielle Steel

'We're friends. I'm helping him remodel the house, by telling him how it used to be.'

'Why can't you stay at a hotel?'

'Because I'd rather stay at the château, and he wants me there. He says it will save him a lot of time.'

'I think you're taking a hell of a chance,' Billy said, sounding worried. 'What if he jumps on you, or makes a pass at you? You're alone with him in the house.'

'He's not going to do that, I promise you. And he has friends coming down for the weekend.' On the one hand he was pleased for her, but on the other, Billy thought she was being very foolish to trust the man. But the more he said, the more she laughed at him, and she was suddenly sounding very French.

'Just be careful, for God's sake. You don't even know who he is, except that he's living in your old house. That's not enough.'

'He's a very respectable man.' She was quick to defend Bernard.

'There's no such thing,' Billy said suspiciously, but she sounded happy and independent, and so pleased to be back home. And it was obvious to

148

both of them, from what she said, and so evidently felt, that to her it was still home. She told him about Sophie's letters then, and he said he wasn't surprised. It sounded like just the kind of thing her Aunt Carole would have done. 'Anyway, be careful, and let me know how you are.'

'I will. But don't worry about me, Billy. I'm fine.' And he could certainly hear that she was. 'I miss you.' That was true, and he missed her too. And now more than ever, he was worried about her.

She went back to the château, and that night she and Bernard went out again. And the following morning, his friends arrived. They were a lively group, the women were sophisticated and fashionable, and all of them were well dressed, and extremely nice to Marie-Ange. Bernard explained who she was, and that she and her family had lived at the château when she was a child. One of the men recognized her name, and knew of her father's enterprise. He commented that John Hawkins had been an extremely respected and successful man. She told Bernard how her parents had met, and he was touched by it, but even more impressed by what his friend had said about her father's success in exporting wines. And she realized that men were more intrigued by business than romance.

It was an idyllic weekend for all of them, and when she packed her bags after the weekend, Bernard begged her not to go. But she knew she had been there long enough, and had told him all she could about the château. It was definitely time for her to leave, and she wanted to visit the Sorbonne, but she would cherish the memory of the ten days she had spent at Marmouton with him, and she thanked him profusely before she left, and was touched when he kissed her on both cheeks and told her how sad he was to see her go.

She drove back to Paris that day, and had dinner alone at her hotel, thinking of him, and the days she had just spent in what had once been her family's château. It was a precious gift Bernard had given her, and she was deeply grateful to him. The next day, she wrote him a long thank-you note, as she sat at the Deux Magots. She mailed it that night. In the morning she went to the Sorbonne to see about classes. She still hadn't decided whether to enroll, or go back to Iowa to finish her last year of college there. And she was thinking seriously about it, as she took a walk along the Boulevard Saint-Germain that afternoon to decide what to do, and ran smack into Bernard de Beauchamp on her way back to her hotel.

'What are you doing here?' she asked with a look of surprise. 'I thought you were staying in Marmouton.'

'I was,' he said sheepishly. 'But I came to Paris to see you. The place was like a tomb once you left.' She was touched and flattered by what he said, and assumed he had other things to do in town, but she was as happy to see him as he was to see her.

He took her to Lucas Carton for dinner that night, and Chez Laurent the next day for lunch, and she told him all about her visit to the Sorbonne. And he begged her to come back to Marmouton with him, for a few days at least, and after resisting for as long as she thought reasonable, she finally packed her bags and went. She had given up her rented car by then, and drove back down to Marmouton with him, and was amazed by how much she enjoyed his company, and how much there always was to say. They were never bored for an instant talking to each other,

and when they reached Marmouton, she felt as
though she had come home.

She stayed there for a week the second time, and
they grew more comfortable with each other every
day, as they walked in the woods, and spent hours
wandering the grounds.

It was nearly the end of the month when she
went back to her hotel in Paris finally, and he went
back to his house there after a few days, and came
to see her at her hotel. They were together constantly, for meals, and long walks in the Bois de
Boulogne. She was more comfortable with him
than she had been with anyone in a long time.
Other than Billy in Iowa, Bernard had become her
only friend. And the only thing that worried
her was deciding what to do about the Sorbonne.
She was having a hard time making up her
mind. She wasn't sure if she should go back to
Iowa, or stay in France.

They were sitting at the Tuileries, when she
brought up the subject. 'I have a better idea, of
something else you should do before you decide,'
he said cryptically. She had no idea what he would
suggest, and was stunned when he suggested she
come to London with him. He had some business

to do there. 'We can go to the theater, and have dinner at Harry's Bar, dance at Annabel's. Marie-Ange, it will do you good. And afterward, we can go to Marmouton for the weekend and then you can decide what to do.' It was as though she had suddenly become swept up in his life. And there was no romance between them, they were just good friends.

In the end, feeling ever more comfortable with him, she went to London, and they stayed in separate rooms at Claridge's, and went out every night. She loved the people they saw, the plays he took her to. They looked at antiques for Marmouton, and went to an auction at Sotheby's. She had a fantastic time with Bernard, and this time, she didn't call Billy to tell him where she was. She was sure he wouldn't understand. And even she knew that it was a bit of a jet-set life, and probably a crazy thing to do, but she had nothing else to do, and Bernard had behaved impeccably. He had never laid a hand on her, and he obviously respected her. They were nothing more than friends until the night they danced at Annabel's, and after dancing with her all night, he leaned down gently and kissed her lips, as she looked up

153

Danielle Steel

at him and wondered what it meant. She would have liked to discuss it with someone, but there was no one she could talk to about Bernard. She could hardly call Billy and consult with him.

But Bernard himself explained it to her when they returned to Marmouton for the weekend. She could sense something different this time, as they walked hand in hand in the woods.

'Marie-Ange, I'm falling in love with you,' he said quietly, with a look of concern. 'This has never happened to me since I lost my wife, and I don't want anyone to get hurt.' As she looked at him, her heart went out to him, and she realized that they were becoming more than just 'friends.' 'Does that sound insane to you? That it should happen so soon?' he asked her with worried eyes. 'I'm so much older than you. I have no right to pull you into my life, particularly if you want to go back to America. But I find that all I want now is to be with you. How do you feel about that?'

'Very touched,' she said cautiously. 'I never thought you would feel that way, Bernard.' He was so sophisticated, and so glamorous, she was flattered to think that he was falling in love with

154

her, and she realized that she was beginning to feel a great deal more for him as well. She had never let herself think about it before, because she had been so determined that they were only friends. But he had not only opened his heart to her, but his home as well. She had imposed on him mercilessly, staying at the château with him, and now all she wanted was to be there with him. She couldn't help wondering if this was the life she had been destined for, and the man.

'What are we going to do about this, my love?' he asked her with such tenderness in his eyes that this time when he kissed her beneath the tree where she had played as a child, she was no longer surprised.

'I don't know. I've never been in love before,' she admitted to him. She was not only a virgin physically, but emotionally as well. There had never been a serious love in her life until then, and suddenly everything was new to her, and more than a little dazzling, like Bernard himself.

'Perhaps we should give it a little time,' he said sensibly. But from that moment on sensible seemed to be impossible for either of them.

They stayed at Marmouton for longer than they

had planned, and he brought her flowers, and small thoughtful gifts, they kissed constantly, and Bernard was so passionately in love with her that Marie-Ange was swept away on the wave of all that she felt for him as well. And finally he made love to her for the first time, in November, just a little over a month after they'd met. And as they lay in each other's arms afterward, he said all the things that she had never dared to dream she would hear from any man.

'I want to marry you,' he whispered to her, 'I want to have children with you. I want to be with you all the time we can.' He told her, having lost a wife and son, he knew how ephemeral life could be, and he didn't want to lose a single moment this time. And Marie-Ange had never been as happy in her life. 'This isn't respectable, Marie-Ange,' he complained to her finally. He was worried about her. 'I'm a forty-year-old man, you're still a very young girl. I don't like the kind of things people will say about you, if they discover that we're having an affair. It's not fair to you.' He looked distressed, and she looked panicked, thinking that he was ending their romance. But he clarified it immediately, much to her relief. 'You have no family to lend you respectability. You're completely at my mercy, and alone in the world.'

'I think being "at your mercy" is very nice,' she teased.

'Well, I don't. If you had a family to protect you, it would be a different story. But you don't.'

'So what do you suggest? Do you want to adopt me?' She was smiling once she knew that he was not ending it with her. She loved the way he worried about her, and wanted to protect her. No one had ever done that before, except Billy, and he was only a boy. Bernard was very much a man. He was old enough to be her father, and he acted like one sometimes. But having lost her own at such an early age, she loved the protection he offered, and his obvious concern. She was totally in love with him.

'I don't want to adopt you, Marie-Ange,' he said solemnly, almost reverently, as she reached out and touched his hand. 'I want to marry you. I don't think we should wait much longer. We haven't known each other for long, but we know each other better than most people who get married after five years. We have no secrets from each other, we've been together almost every instant since we met. Marie-Ange,' he looked at her tenderly, 'I love you more than I've ever loved anyone in my life.'

'I love you too, Bernard,' she said softly, amazed by what he was suggesting. It had all happened so quickly, but it seemed so perfectly right to her too. There was no more thought of school. Just Bernard and returning to the château – and having a family. He was offering her a life that seemed more like a dream.

'Let's get married this week. Here, in Marmouton. We can be married in the chapel, and then begin our life together. It will be a new start for both of us,' and one they both wanted more than anything or anyone else. 'Will you?'

'I . . . yes . . . I will.' He held her close for a long time, and then they walked back to the house hand in hand. They made love for hours that afternoon. And he called the priest and made the arrangements the next day. And after he did, she called Billy, from the château this time. At first, she had no idea what to tell him, and in the end, she just blurted it out. She was worried about hurting him, although she had always discouraged him from having romantic thoughts about her.

But she knew how much he cared about her.

'You're doing *what*?' Billy shouted at her in disbelief. 'I thought you were just friends.' He sounded horrified by what she had told him, and he accused her of losing her mind since she arrived in France. She had never been impulsive before, but she was madly in love with Bernard, and he was a powerful force now in her life, a man with passion and determination and a forceful way about him. He had completely swept Marie-Ange off her feet in an incredibly short time.

'We were just friends, but things changed,' she said in a small voice. She hadn't expected him to be quite as upset as he was.

'Apparently. Look, Marie-Ange, just give it some time, and see if this is real. You just got there, it was emotional for you, going back to the château. It's all wrapped up in that.' He was pleading with her.

'No, it's not,' she insisted. 'It's him.' He didn't want to ask her if she was sleeping with him, he had already guessed that she was. And she absolutely wouldn't listen to him. He was worried sick about her when he got off the phone, but he knew there was nothing he could do. She was marrying a perfect stranger, Billy thought, mostly because he was living in her father's château. And what's more, he was a count. He felt utterly helpless to change her mind.

'Who was that?' Bernard asked her when she got off the phone.

'My best friend in Iowa.' She smiled at him. 'He thinks I've lost my mind.' She was sorry to have upset Billy, but she was entirely sure of Bernard, and his love for her, and hers for him.

'So have I.' Bernard smiled. 'It must be contagious.'

'What did the priest say?' she asked calmly. She wasn't worried about any of the things Billy said. He was suspicious of Bernard, understandably, and only time would prove him wrong. But she had wanted him to know that she and Bernard were getting married. He was, after all, her best friend, and like a brother to her. In the end, he had said to call him if she came to her senses, or even if she didn't. And he promised her that he would always be her friend, and be there for her. But as much as she loved him, she needed him less now. She had been completely absorbed in Bernard's heady world, and she couldn't help wondering what his friends would think, but he didn't seem to care. They were both absolutely certain that they were doing the right thing.

'The priest said we will do the civil ceremony at the *mairie* in two days, on Friday, and he will marry us at the chapel here the next day. He's going to publish the banns today and shorten the waiting period a bit. How does that sound to you, Madame la Comtesse?' She hadn't even thought of that. She would be a countess now. It really was like a fairy tale. Four months before, she had been Aunt Carole's slave, and then a month later, she had become an heiress with an enormous fortune, and now she was marrying a count who adored her, and whom she adored, and returning to her family home in Marmouton. Her head spun as she thought about it, and it was still spinning when they went to the *mairie* together two days later to be civilly married. And the next day, they stood in the chapel on their property, and were married in the eyes of God. Madame Fournier and Alain were their witnesses, and the old woman cried through the entire ceremony, thanking God that Marie-Ange had come home.

'I love you, my darling,' Bernard said as he

kissed her after the ceremony, and the priest smiled. They made a handsome couple, the Comte and Comtesse de Beauchamp.

And when the priest and the Fourniers left them, after drinking champagne with them, Bernard swept her into his arms and took her upstairs to the guest suite he used as his bedroom at the château, and he laid her gently on the bed in the pretty white silk dress she had worn. He ran a hand over her golden hair and then kissed her again. 'I adore you,' he whispered, and Marie-Ange kissed him, hardly able to believe all that had happened to her, or how happy she was. And he gently took her dress off, as he peeled away his own clothes, and when he made love to her that night, all he hoped was that he would make her happy and that she would conceive his child.

Chapter Nine

Their first Christmas together at the château was blissful. Bernard was so obviously in love with her that it made people smile to watch them together. And being back in the château at Christmas again brought back a million memories for her, some of them beautiful, and some of them finally less painful, because he was with her. She talked to Billy in Iowa on Christmas Eve, and he was happy for her, but still worried that she didn't know her husband well enough and had been too impulsive about getting married. And she reassured him as best she could. She had never been as happy in her life.

'Who would have thought a year ago that I'd have been living in Marmouton again this

Christmas?' she said dreamily to Billy on the phone, and he smiled wistfully, remembering the time they had spent together. He was still recovering from the shock of knowing that she was married now, and not coming back to Iowa, except maybe for a visit someday. He was seeing a lot of his girlfriend Debbi, but missing Marie-Ange. Nothing was the same anymore.

'Who would have thought a year ago that you'd turn out to be an heiress, and I'd be driving a new Porsche?' In some ways it seemed fitting even to him that she would be a countess. And he hoped for her that Bernard would turn out to be everything she thought he was. But Billy was still leery of him. It had all happened so quickly.

Life continued in the same fast pace for Bernard and Marie-Ange after the holidays. They traveled back and forth to Paris and stayed at his apartment. It was small but beautiful and filled with wonderful antiques. In January, she discovered she was pregnant, and Bernard was ecstatic. He kept talking about how old he was, how much he wanted a child with her, and that he hoped it would be an heir for his title. He desperately wanted a son.

And within days of her announcing to him that their first child was on the way, the renovation on Marmouton began, and within weeks the château was a shambles. Suddenly, they were redoing everything, the roof, the walls, the long French windows were being enlarged, the height of the doorways. He had a spectacular new kitchen planned, a brand-new master suite for them, a nursery that he promised her would look like a fairy tale, and a movie theater in the basement. The entire electrical system was being revamped, along with the plumbing. It was a massive undertaking that far exceeded Marie-Ange's understanding of what he'd planned, and it was easy to figure out that it was going to be staggeringly expensive. He was even planting endless acres of new vineyards and orchards. But Bernard told Marie-Ange that he wanted her home to be perfect for her. The work was being designed by his architect friend from Paris. And there were dozens of workers everywhere.

And Bernard also promised her that much of the interior work would be done by the time she had the baby in September. And when she called Billy again, she told him she was pregnant.

Danielle Steel

'You sure didn't waste any time, did you?' he said, still sounding worried about her. Everything seemed to be happening to her with the speed of sound, and she told him that Bernard was anxious to start a family with her, as he was so much older than she was, and had lost his only son.

She had also written to her Aunt Carole to tell her about the changes in her life, but she had had no answer. It was as though her great-aunt had closed the door on her and moved on.

By March, the château was covered with scaffolding, there were workmen everywhere, and they spent more time in Paris. And although Bernard's apartment was small for both of them, it was a splendid pied-à-terre, with grand reception rooms, high ceilings, and beautiful old *boiseries* and wood paneling. It was filled with expensive antiques, paintings he had inherited from his family, and Aubusson carpets. It was indeed an apartment fit for a countess. But they both preferred Marmouton.

And in the summer, he told her that they needed to get away from the construction at the château, and their absence would allow the workmen to move faster. He had rented a villa in Saint-Jean-

Cap-Ferrat for them, and a 200-foot motor yacht that went with it. And he had invited a number of his friends to visit them there.

'My God, Bernard, how you spoil me!' She laughed when she saw the house and yacht in Saint-Jean-Cap-Ferrat. They had them for the month of July, and by August they planned to be in Marmouton again, as by then, she would be eight months pregnant, and wanted to slow down. She was going to have the baby at the hospital in Poitiers.

The time they spent in the South of France seemed like magic to her. They went out, saw his friends, and the villa was constantly filled with houseguests from Rome, Munich, London, and Paris. And everyone who visited them saw how happy they were and was delighted for them.

Her time with Bernard had been the happiest nine months of her life, and they were both excited about the baby. The nursery was ready when they got back to Marmouton, and Bernard had hired a local girl as a nanny for her. And their sumptuous master suite was completed for them at the end of August, but the rest of the château was still a work in progress. But so far, despite the amount of work they'd done, there hadn't been a single problem. Everything was going according to plan.

It was on the morning of September first, as she was folding tiny little shirts in the nursery, that the local contractor came to find her. He said he had some questions to ask her about the ongoing work on the plumbing. Bernard had put in fabulous new marble bathrooms, with jacuzzis, enormous tubs, and even several saunas.

But she was startled when, at the end of his conversation with her, the contractor seemed reluctant to leave the room and looked awkward. There was obviously something on his mind, and when she asked him pointedly what it was, he told her.

His bills had not been paid since the work began, although the count had promised him a payment in March, and another larger one in August. And all of the other suppliers who were working for them were encountering the same problem. She wondered if Bernard simply hadn't had time to get to it, or had forgotten while they were on the Riviera. But what she discovered, as she questioned the man, was that no one had been paid since the beginning of the project. And when she asked him if he had an idea of what was currently owed to them, he told her he wasn't sure, but that it was well over a million dollars. She stared at him in astonishment as he told her the numbers. She had never thought to ask Bernard what he was paying to restore the château, and even improve it. When he was through, it was going to be impeccable outside, and state of the art inside. But it had never occurred to her what it would cost him to restore the château for her.

'Are you sure?' Marie-Ange asked the contractor in disbelief. 'It can't be that much.' How could it be? How could it possibly cost that much to redo the château? She was embarrassed that Bernard was planning to spend that much on it, and felt guilty for all the changes she had approved. And she promised the contractor to discuss it with her husband that night, when he got back from a brief business trip to Paris. He hadn't actually worked in the past year, although he went to Paris for meetings several times a month, but she knew that they were to meet with his advisers on his own investments. He had told her he was loath to go back to working at the bank, he wanted to spend time with her, and concentrate on the construction they were doing. And in the fall, he wanted to spend more time with her and the baby, and she was flattered and pleased that he wanted to do that.

But that night, when he got home, she mentioned her meeting with the contractor, and was embarrassed to bother him about it. She said simply that some of the suppliers had not been paid, and she wondered if his Paris secretary had somehow forgotten to send the payments. And much to her relief, Bernard didn't seem worried about it. She also told him how sorry she was that the renovation was costing him so dearly.

'It's worth every penny of it, my love,' he said with a tenderness and ease that touched her deeply. He begrudged her nothing. In fact, he constantly spoiled her, with small gifts and large ones. He had bought a beautiful Jaguar for her in June, and himself a new Bentley. And he told her now that he had been waiting for some investments to clear before he paid the contractor a large balloon payment. He had told her he was heavily invested in oil in the Middle East, and he had other holdings in a variety of countries, and he didn't want to lose money selling them while the various international markets fluctuated. It sounded perfectly sensible to her, as it would have to anyone, she assumed. In fact, he said, with a look of mild embarrassment, he had been thinking about asking her to use some of her funds temporarily, as everything she had was fairly liquid, and he would repay her when some of his investments matured, in early October. It was a matter of a month or six weeks, but would satisfy their creditors, and Marie-Ange saw no problem with it. She told him to do whatever he wanted to handle it, she trusted him completely. He said he'd handle it with her bank, and would have her sign whatever was needed to make the transfers. But she was still apologetic to him about what it would eventually cost him, and offered to alter some of what they'd planned so it would be less expensive.

'Don't worry your pretty head about it, my love. I want everything to be perfect for you. All you have to think about is having the baby.' Which was what she did for the next two weeks. She put the entire matter of the construction bills out of her mind, particularly after he had her sign the papers to make the transfer from her account to his. And the contractor assured her the following week that everyone was satisfied now. It didn't even worry her that she had advanced $1,500,000 to cover it, because Bernard was going to reimburse her shortly. It still amazed her to be talking about that kind of money, and she had assured the head of the trust department at her bank, when he questioned her, that it was only a temporary transfer.

She spent the next two weeks taking long walks with Bernard in the familiar woods she loved, and going out to dinner with him. Everything at the château was ready for their baby, although the rest of the work still continued.

The baby came on schedule, late one night, and Bernard drove her to Poitiers when the pains got strong enough. He took her to the hospital in style, like a queen, in his new Bentley. And he was pleased that the delivery was quick and easy, and the baby, a little girl, was beautiful and healthy. She was the portrait of her mother. And they named her Heloise, Heloise Françoise Hawkins de Beauchamp, and brought her home two days later.

Marie-Ange fell instantly in love with her, and

Bernard made a huge fuss over both mother and baby. There was champagne and caviar when they got home, and a spectacular diamond bracelet for Marie-Ange for being so brave, he said, and because he was so proud of her. But he also let her know that he hoped that Heloise would have a little brother soon. He still desperately wanted a son and heir for his title, and although he never actually said it to her, Marie-Ange had a lingering suspicion that she had failed him.

And when Heloise was a month old, the contractor came to see Marie-Ange, and told her that the bills had not been paid for the past six weeks, and had mounted up again. This time they amounted to roughly $250,000

His request reminded Marie-Ange that Bernard's holdings were about to mature then, and she mentioned it to him, hesitantly, but with no doubt that he would pay for the continuing work at Marmouton, which was due to be complete by Christmas. And Bernard assured her that it was not a problem, although the maturity on his investments had been extended again, and he needed her to cover the bills just one more time, and he would pay her all of it in November. She explained it to her bank, as she had before, and the following day made the transfer. She had paid out nearly $2,000,000 by then, but the Château de Marmouton had never looked better.

And when Heloise was six weeks old, Marie-Ange surprised Bernard by visiting him in Paris. But when she got to the apartment, he was not there, and the woman who cleaned for them told her that he was at the rue de Varenne, overseeing the workers there.

'What workers? What is at the rue de Varenne?' Marie-Ange looked startled, and the woman looked worried. She said she thought it might be a surprise for Marie-Ange, and they had only begun construction the week before. She suggested that Marie-Ange not say anything to her husband about it, but Marie-Ange couldn't resist the urge to drive by the address and see what was there. And what she saw when she drove by, with the baby in the car with her, was an enormous eighteenth-century *hôtel particulier*, with stables, a huge garden, and a courtyard. And Bernard was standing out front with the architect and an armload of blueprints, and before she could drive away again, they saw her.

'So you found it,' he beamed at her. 'I was going to surprise you with the blueprints at Christmas.' He looked proud rather than disappointed that she had found him. And Marie-Ange looked baffled.

'What is this?' Marie-Ange asked, feeling confused, as the baby began to cry in the backseat. It was time to nurse her.

'Your house in Paris, my love,' he said tenderly to her, as he kissed her. 'Come in and take a look, now that you're here.' It was the most beautiful house she'd ever seen, and a very large one, but it was also obvious that it hadn't been touched in years, and had been maintained very badly. 'I got it for almost nothing.'

'Bernard,' she whispered in astonishment, 'can we afford this?'

'I think so,' he said confidently. 'Don't you? I'd say it's the appropriate city residence for the Comte and Comtesse de Beauchamp.' To Marie-Ange, it looked as though Marie-Antoinette had lived there. And as Bernard walked her around, he said there was even some question that one of the earlier Comtes de Beauchamp might have owned it. It was pure kismet that they had found it.

'When did you buy it?'

'Just before you had the baby,' he admitted to her with a boyish smile. 'I wanted to surprise you.' But what worried her was that the work at Marmouton wasn't even finished, nor paid for. But Bernard seemed to have no fear of spending money. And she assumed that he had more than enough to back it, although none of his assets were liquid.

They spent the night in the apartment in Paris, and he was attentive and charming, and by the end of the evening he had almost convinced her that it would be a good place for him to work when he came to town, and to entertain friends who didn't want to travel to Marmouton to see them.

'And now we can spend time in both places,' he said proudly. The house on the rue de Varenne was so elegant, he pointed out, that it even had a ball-room. But Marie-Ange was still uneasy when they drove back to the château the next morning.

'Can we really afford all that?' Marie-Ange asked, looking worried. For the first time she had the feeling that they were spending too much money.

'I think so. And our little system seems to work perfectly, with you advancing me small sums to juggle minor bills, and I have the time to handle our investments correctly.' The only problem was that the investments were his, and the 'small sums' she had advanced to him were nearly $2,000,000. But she could only assume that he knew what he was doing, and she trusted him completely.

By Christmas, the château was nearly complete, and the best gift she gave him that year was telling him on Christmas Eve that she was pregnant again, and she hoped it would be a boy this time so he wouldn't be disappointed.

'Nothing you could ever do would disappoint me,' he said generously. But they both knew that he wanted a son desperately. Heloise was three and a half months old by then, and the new baby was due in August, there would be eleven months between the two children. As always, things were moving at lightning speed between them. And this time she didn't call Billy to tell him the news, she sent him a letter with her Christmas card. She only called him every month or two now. She was so engrossed in her life with Bernard that she scarcely had time to think of anything else, except her baby.

But in January, when Marie-Ange made a large transfer from her bank to Bernard's again, the head of the trust department called her.

'Is everything all right, Marie-Ange? You're starting to go through your money like water.' There was certainly enough there not to worry about it excessively, but with the latest transfer to pay for work on the Paris house, she had spent just over $2,000,000. She had nearly a £1,500,000 left available to her, until she turned twenty-five and inherited the next installment, but the head of the trust department was concerned about her. And she explained to him the system she and Bernard had, of her advancing money for things, and his reimbursing her at the right time from his investments.

'And when will that be?' the head of the trust department asked primly.

'Very soon,' she assured him. 'He is paying for all the work on both houses.' He had never said precisely that to her, but he had certainly implied it, and she felt confident in reassuring her banker.

But the following week, Bernard explained to

her that there was an oil crisis in the Middle East and he would lose untold sums if he tried to cash out his investments. It was far wiser for him to continue to hold them, and in the end, it would make them a great deal of money. But that also meant that she needed to pay a million-dollar deposit immediately, for what they owed on the house in Paris. He assured her that they had bought it for a song, and had three years to pay the previous owner the remaining $2,000,000, and she would have inherited the next installment of her trust by then.

'I don't get the next installment of my inheritance until I turn twenty-five,' she told Bernard with a look of concern. It was a little frightening to her to be the upfront banker for him, particularly on the scale that he was used to. But he kissed her and smiled at her, and said one of the things he loved about her was her innocence.

'Trusts like yours, my love, can easily be broken. You're a responsible married woman, with a child, and a second one on the way. What we are doing here is making a sensible investment, not gambling at Monte Carlo. And the officers of your trust will be reasonable about it. They can either invade the trust for you, or advance you money against the next installment you're getting. In point of fact, directly or otherwise, the entire amount of the trust is available to you. How much is it, by the way?' He asked casually, and Marie-Ange didn't hesitate to tell him.

'A little more than ten million dollars in total.'

'That's a nice amount,' he said, seemingly unimpressed, and it was easy to deduce from that, that his own investments were far larger, but he was also twenty years older than she was, had had a successful career, and came from an illustrious family. He was not impressed by what she had, but he was satisfied for her that what her father had left her was respectable certainly, and he was pleased for her. 'We'll talk to your bankers about your access to it, whenever you want to.' He seemed to know a great deal about those matters, and Marie-Ange was intrigued by what he told her, and less worried.

By late spring, he had not repaid her yet, and she was embarrassed to ask him again, but at least she had paid off everything at Marmouton, and all she had to think about now was the work on the house in Paris. Although what Bernard had planned for it was certainly grandiose, he assured her that in the end, the house would be a historical monument, and a permanent legacy for their children. On that basis, it was hard to deny him, and she didn't.

They spent July in the South of France again, with a larger yacht, and the usual army of visiting friends, but this time Marie-Ange felt less well before the birth of her baby. They were moving around a lot, between Paris and the château, over-seeing the work of Herculean proportions they were doing in Paris, and Bernard had taken her to Venice for a party, the week before they left the South of France. And she was tired when they finally got back to Marmouton. The weather was hot, and she could hardly wait for the baby to come. This one was far larger than the first one.

It came, in the end, a week after it was due, and she and Bernard were spending a quiet weekend at the château. And this time she managed to fulfill his dreams. The baby was a boy, and although she didn't say it to him, she hoped that he would make up for his lost son. Bernard was ecstatic over him,

181

and even more so over her. They named the baby
after her brother Robert.

Marie-Ange recovered more slowly this time,
the birth had been difficult, because the baby was
bigger than Heloise had been, but by mid-
September she was back in Paris with Bernard,
overseeing the work at the house on the rue de
Varenne. She hadn't said anything to Bernard
about it, but he had never reimbursed her for a
penny of the funds she had advanced to him, and
she had given him every cent she had available to
her through her trust, and the bills were continuing to roll in without mercy. She assumed Bernard
would take care of them eventually, along with the
funds he owed her.

She was in Paris, at the new house, and had
both of her children with her, when the architect
surprised her by what he said. Bernard had told
her categorically that he wasn't buying anything
for the house, until they had paid their existing
bills. And the architect mentioned to her that
there was a storage room near Les Halles that
Bernard was filling with the things he was continuing to buy for them, mostly paintings and
priceless antiques. She asked Bernard about it that

night, and he denied it, and said he couldn't imagine why the architect had said a thing like that, but when she checked his files the next day when Bernard went out, she found a fat file full of bills from art galleries and antique stores. The file contained yet another million dollars' worth of bills. And she still had the file in her hand, when the phone rang. Billy was calling her to congratulate her on the birth of Robert.

'How's everything going over there?' he asked, sounding happy. 'Is he still Prince Charming?' he inquired, and she insisted that he was, but she was distracted over the disturbing file of bills she was holding. What upset her most was that he had lied about it, and written right on the top of the file was the address of the storage facility he said they didn't have. It was the first time she had ever caught him in a lie. And she said nothing to Billy about it. She didn't want to be disloyal to Bernard.

Billy said he had heard that her Aunt Carole had been sick, and more important, he told Marie-Ange he was getting married. His fiancée was the same girl he had been going out with when Marie-Ange left, and she was happy for him. They were planning to be married the following summer.

'Well, since you wouldn't marry me, Marie-Ange,' he teased her, 'I had no choice but to go out and fend for myself.' His fiancée was finishing college herself that year, and they were hoping to get married after she graduated. He told Marie-Ange he hoped she'd come, and she said she'd try to. But she'd been so nervous about the pile of bills she'd found that for once she didn't enjoy talking to Billy. She was still thinking about Billy when she hung up, and of how wonderful it would be to see him again. But as much as she loved him, she had her own life now, a husband and family. She had her hands full, and she was worried about their mountain of unpaid bills. She wasn't sure how to broach the subject to Bernard, and needed some time to think about it. She was sure that there was some explanation of why he had been less than honest with her about the things he had in storage. Maybe he wanted to surprise her. She wanted to believe that his motive had been a good one, and she didn't want a confrontation with him.

She still hadn't broached the subject to him when they went back to Marmouton the following week, when she made a discovery there that truly shocked her. A bill had come to him for an expensive ruby ring that had been delivered to someone at a Paris address. And the woman who bought it was using Bernard's last name. It was the second time in a matter of a week that Marie-Ange began doubting him, and she was obsessed by her own terrors. She was so frightened of what it meant, thinking that he'd been unfaithful to her, that she decided to drive to Paris with her babies. Bernard was in London visiting friends and taking care of some of his investments, and she stayed at the apartment in Paris, while she pondered the problem.

Marie-Ange felt terribly guilty, but she called her bank and asked them to refer her to a private investigator. She felt like a traitor when she called, but she needed to know what Bernard was doing, and if he was cheating on her. He certainly had ample opportunity to do it, when he was in Paris, or elsewhere, but she had always been so convinced that he loved her. She wondered if this woman was a girlfriend of his, and had been brazen enough to use his name and pretend to be married to him. Or far more happily, maybe it was only a coincidence of last names, she was a distant relative, and her purchase had found its way onto Bernard's bill entirely by mistake. She wasn't sure what to believe or how it had happened, and she didn't want to expose herself by asking the store for information. It broke her heart now to doubt him, but given the amount of money he was spending, and the ruby ring she couldn't account for, she knew she needed some answers.

Marie-Ange still wanted to believe there was an acceptable explanation for it, perhaps the woman who had bought the ring was psychotic. But whatever the explanation for the ring, she was still worried about why he had lied to her about the items in storage. And none of it solved the problem of the unpaid bills that were accruing. They could be dealt with at least, but what she wanted to know most was that she could trust him. She didn't want to discuss any of it with him until she knew more. If the matter of the ring was all an innocent mistake, and the things in the storage vault were a surprise for her, gifts he intended to pay for himself, then she didn't want to accuse him. But if something different surfaced in her investigations, then she would have to face Bernard with it, and hear his side of the story.

In the meantime, she wanted to believe the best of him, but there was a gnawing fear in her heart. She had always trusted him, and thrown herself wholeheartedly into her life with him. They had had two babies in less than two years. But the fact was that she had ended up paying entirely for the renovations at the château, and now at the house on the rue de Varenne. All told, they had spent $3,000,000 of her money to do it, they owed another $2,000,000 on the house in Paris, and there were more than $1,000,000 currently in unpaid bills. It was a staggering amount of money to have spent in less than two years. And Bernard had not yet put the brakes on his spending.

As Marie-Ange walked into the investigator's office, she felt her heart sink. It was small and seamy and dirty, and the investigator the bank had referred her to looked disheveled, and was unfriendly, as he jotted down some notes and asked her some very personal questions. And as she listened to herself reel off facts and houses and dollar amounts, it was easy to see why she was worried. But spending too much money did not make Bernard a liar. It was the bill for the ruby ring that most upset her, and that she wanted to question. Why was the woman who had received it using Bernard's last name? Marie-Ange had been told by Bernard that none of his relatives were living. But as concerned as she was about it, she still believed that there was possibly a simple and innocent explanation. It was not impossible that there was another person in France, unrelated to him, who had the same last name.

'Do you want me to check for any other unpaid bills?' the investigator asked, assuming that she would, and she nodded. She had already expressed her concerns about the woman and the ring. But she just couldn't imagine that Bernard would cheat on her, and buy an expensive gift for his mistress, and then expect Marie-Ange to pay the bill. No one could be that bold or that tasteless. Certainly not Bernard. He was sensitive and elegant and honest, Marie-Ange believed.

'I don't really think there is a problem,' Marie-Ange apologized for her suspicions, 'I just got worried when I found the file of unpaid bills, and the storage room he hadn't told me about . . . and now the ring . . . I don't know who the woman could be, or why the bill came to my husband. It's probably a mistake.'

'I understand,' the investigator said, without judgment, and then he looked up and smiled at her.

'In your shoes, I'd be worried too. That's an awful lot of money to pour out in under two years.' It was staggering, and he was amazed she'd let him do it. But she was young, and naive, and he correctly guessed that her husband was a master at it.

'Well, of course, it's all been an investment,' Marie-Ange explained. 'Our houses are wonderful, and they're both historical.' She said the same things to him that her husband had said to her, to justify the expenses and the cost of the restorations. But she was afraid now that there might be more she didn't know. He had never told her about the house in Paris, until after he bought it and had begun work on it, and she couldn't help wondering now what else he had concealed from her.

But she was in no way prepared for what the investigator told her after he called her in Marmouton. He asked her if she wanted to meet with him in Paris, or if she would prefer that he come to the château. Bernard was in Paris, and

Danielle Steel

Robert was only six weeks old, but had a bad cold, and she suggested that the investigator come to see her.

He arrived the following morning, and she led him into the office that Bernard used when he was there. She could read nothing from the man's expression, and she offered him a cup of coffee, but he declined it. He wanted to get right down to business with her, and took a file from his briefcase, as he looked across the desk at Marie-Ange, and she suddenly had the odd feeling that she should brace herself for what he would say.

'You were right to be worried about the bills,' he told her without preamble. 'There are another six hundred thousand dollars of unpaid bills, most of which he spent on paintings and clothes.'

'Clothes for whom?' she asked, looking puzzled and worried as she thought of the ruby ring again, but the investigator rapidly put that fear to rest.

'Himself. He has a very expensive tailor in London, and a hundred thousand dollars' worth of outstanding bills at Hermès. The rest is all art objects, antiques, I assume for your houses. And the ruby ring was purchased by a woman called

190

Louise de Beauchamp. In fact, the bill went to your husband in error,' he said simply, as Marie-Ange beamed at him from across the desk. The bills could be paid eventually, or if they had to, the art objects could be sold. But a mistress would have been a different problem, and Marie-Ange would have been heartbroken. She didn't even care about the rest of what the investigator had to say to her, he had already acquitted Bernard, and she was ashamed of the suspicions that she'd had about him. 'What was interesting about Louise de Beauchamp, when I found her,' the investigator went on, despite Marie-Ange's broad smile and sudden lack of concern, 'is that your husband married her seven years ago. I assume you didn't know that or you'd have told me.'

'That's impossible,' Marie-Ange said, looking at him strangely. 'His wife and son died in a fire twelve years ago, and their son was four. This woman must be lying,' unless he'd had a brief marriage after he'd lost them, and never told Marie-Ange, but it was so unlike Bernard to lie to her, or so she thought.

'That's not entirely correct,' the investigator continued, almost sorry for her. 'Louise de

Beauchamp's son died in that fire, but it was five years ago. The boy was not your husband's son, he was hers by a prior marriage. And she survived. It was only a fluke that she happened to buy that ring, and it was mistakenly charged to your husband's account. She showed me documents to prove his marriage to her, and clippings about the fire. He collected insurance on the château that burned down. It was purchased with funds from her, but it was in his name. And I believe he used the insurance money to buy this one. But he had no funds to remodel it until you came along,' he said bluntly to Marie-Ange. 'And he hasn't had a job since he and Louise were married.'

'Does he know she's alive?' she asked, looking utterly confused. It didn't even occur to her that Bernard had lied to her, and that he had been for two years. Somewhere, somehow there had to be an enormous misunderstanding. Bernard would never lie to her.

'I assume he does know she's alive. They were divorced.'

'That can't be. We were married in the Catholic Church.'

'Maybe he paid off the priest,' the investigator

said simply. He had far fewer illusions than Marie-Ange. 'I went to speak to Madame de Beauchamp myself, and she would like to meet with you, if you'd like to. She asked me to warn you not to tell your husband if you do.' He handed Marie-Ange her phone number in Paris, and she saw that the address was on the Avenue Foch, at an excellent address. 'She got badly burned in the fire, and she has scars. I've been told that she lives more or less as a recluse.' The odd thing was that none of Bernard's friends had ever said anything to her about it, nor about the son he had lost. 'I have the feeling that she never got over losing the boy.'

'Neither did he,' Marie-Ange said with eyes full of tears. Now that she had children, the thought of losing a child seemed like the ultimate nightmare to her, and her heart went out to this woman, whoever she was, and whatever her tie had been to Bernard. She still did not believe her story, and wanted to get to the bottom of it. Someone was lying, but surely not Bernard.

'I think you should see her, Comtesse. She has a lot to say about your husband, and perhaps they are things that you should know.'

'Like what?' Marie-Ange asked, looking increasingly disturbed.

'She thinks he set the fire that killed the boy.' He didn't tell Marie-Ange that Louise de Beauchamp thought that Bernard had tried to kill her as well. She could tell Marie-Ange that herself, for whatever it was worth. But the investigator had been impressed by her.

'That's a terrible thing to say.' Marie-Ange looked outraged. 'Perhaps she feels she has to blame someone. Maybe she can't accept the fact that it was an accident and her son died.' But that still didn't explain the fact that she was alive, and that Bernard had never told her the boy wasn't really his son, or that he'd been divorced from this woman. Her mind was suddenly reeling, filled with doubts and questions, and she didn't know if she was grateful or sorry that the investigator had found Louise de Beauchamp. Odd as it seemed, she was relieved that at least she wasn't his mistress. But it was hardly comforting to think she believed he had killed her son. And why was her story so different from Bernard's? She wasn't even sure she wanted to see her, and open that Pandora's box, but after the investigator left her,

Marie-Ange went for a long walk in the orchards, thinking about Louise de Beauchamp and her son.

It was difficult to sort it all out. And she was worried too about how they were going to pay for their bills, and despite Bernard's advice to do it, she didn't want to attempt to overturn her trust and access the rest of her funds. That sounded far too risky to her, particularly if they spent all her money. Leaving her trust intact was at least protection against that.

Her mind was still reeling when she came back from the orchard to feed the baby, and after she put him down in his crib, sated and happy, she stood for a long moment, staring at the phone. She had put the phone number the investigator had given her in her pocket, so Bernard wouldn't find it, and she slowly pulled it out. She thought of calling Billy and talking to him about it, but even that was a disturbing thought. She didn't really know the truth yet, and she didn't want to accuse Bernard unfairly. Maybe he just hadn't wanted to admit that he was divorced, and had loved the boy as his own son. But whatever the truth was, she knew now that she had to know it, and with a shaking hand, picked up the phone to call Louise de Beauchamp.

A deep well-spoken woman's voice answered on the second ring, and Marie-Ange asked for Madame de Beauchamp.

'This is she,' she said calmly, not recognizing the voice at the other end, and Marie-Ange hesitated for a fraction of an instant. It was like looking in the mirror, and being afraid of what you would find there.

'This is Marie-Ange de Beauchamp,' she said in almost a whisper, and there was a small sound at the other end, like a sigh of recognition and relief.

'I wondered if you would call me. I didn't think you would,' she said honestly. 'I'm not sure I would have in your place. But I'm glad you did. There are some things I feel you should know.' She already knew from the investigator that Bernard had never told his young wife about her, and that in itself was further condemnation of him, as far as Louise was concerned. 'Would you like to come and see me? I don't go out,' she said softly. The investigator had told Marie-Ange about the scars on her face. She had had plastic surgery for them, but she had been burned very badly, and there had only been so much the plastic surgeons could repair. The burns had occurred, the investigator told Marie-Ange, while she was trying to save her son.

'I will come to Paris to see you,' Marie-Ange said, with a sick feeling in the pit of her stomach, deathly afraid of what she would be told. Her instincts told her that her faith in her husband was at risk, and part of her wanted to run away and hide, and do anything but meet with Louise de Beauchamp. But she knew she had to. She had no choice. If not, she would always harbor doubts, and she felt she owed it to Bernard to free herself of them. 'When would you like me to come?'

'Is tomorrow too soon for you?' Louise asked gently. She meant her no harm. All she wanted to do for her was save her life. From everything the investigator had told her, she believed that Marie-Ange was in danger, and perhaps her children as well. 'Or the day after tomorrow?' the woman offered, and Marie-Ange answered with a sigh.

'I can drive up tomorrow, and meet you at the end of the day.'

'Is five o'clock too early?'

'No, I can be there. Is it all right if I bring the baby? I'm nursing, and I'll bring him with me from Marmouton.' She was going to leave Heloise with the nanny at the château.

'I'd love to see him,' Louise said kindly, and Marie-Ange thought she could hear a catch in her voice.

'I'll see you at five then,' Marie-Ange promised, wishing she didn't feel she had to go. But there was no choice. She had started out now on this long, lonely road, and she just hoped she would come back safely, with her faith in Bernard restored.

And as she hung up the phone in Paris, Louise looked sadly at a photograph of her little boy, and he was smiling at her. So much had happened since then.

Chapter Ten

The trip from Marmouton to Paris seemed to take forever this time, as Marie-Ange drove with the baby in his car seat, and she had to stop once to nurse him. And outside, it was blustery and cold. It was after four-thirty when she got to Paris, the traffic was heavy, and she got to the address on the Avenue Foch five minutes before her appointment with Louise de Beauchamp. Marie-Ange knew nothing about Bernard's ex-wife, she had never seen a photograph of her, or the boy, which she realized was odd now, but perhaps Bernard had simply wanted to put away the memories of his past life when he married Marie-Ange. What was far more difficult to understand was why she was not dead, as he had told her, but alive.

She had no idea what to expect when the door opened, and she was startled when she saw her. She was a tall, elegant young woman in her late thirties, her hair was blond and hung to her shoulders, and when she moved, her hair seemed to obscure part of her face. But as she opened the door, Marie-Ange saw clearly what had happened to her. On one side of her face, the features were exquisite and delicate, on the other they appeared to have melted, and the surgeries and skin grafts had left ugly scars. Their attempts to repair the burns had failed.

'Thank you for coming, Comtesse,' she said, looking aristocratic but vulnerable, as she turned the damaged side of her face away. She led Marie-Ange into a living room filled with priceless antiques, and they sat down quietly on two Louis XV chairs, as Marie-Ange held her baby, and he slept peacefully in her arms.

Louise de Beauchamp smiled when she saw him, but it was obvious to Marie-Ange that her eyes were filled with grief.

'I don't see babies very often,' she said simply to Marie-Ange. 'I don't see anyone in fact.' And then she offered her something to drink, but

Marie-Ange wanted nothing from her. All she wanted was to listen to what she had to say. 'I know this must be hard for you,' Louise said to her clearly, seeming to gain both her composure and strength as she looked into the young woman's eyes. 'You don't know me. You have no reason to believe me, but I hope that for your sake, and the sake of your children, you will listen, and be watchful from now on.' She took a breath, and then went on, turning her damaged face away again, as Marie-Ange watched her with worried eyes. She didn't look like a crazy person, and although there was an air of sorrow about her, she did not appear bitter or deranged. And she was frighteningly calm as she told her tale.

'We met at a party in Saint-Tropez, and I believe now that Bernard knew full well who I was. My father was a well-known man, he had enormous landholdings all over Europe, and he was involved in oil trades in Bahrain. Bernard knew all of that about me, and also that my father had just died when we met. My mother died when I was a child. I had no relatives, I was alone, and I was young, although not as young as you are now. He courted me passionately and quickly, and he said that all he wanted was to marry me and have a child. I already had a son by an earlier marriage. He was two when I met Bernard. And Charles adored him. Bernard was wonderful with him, and I thought he would be the perfect husband and father. My previous marriage had ended badly, and my ex-husband no longer saw the child. I thought Charles needed a father, and I was very much in love with Bernard. So much so that I included him in my will, after we were married, in equal part to Charles. I thought it was the least I could do for Bernard, and I had no intention of dying for a very long time. But I was foolish enough to tell him what I had done.

'We had a house in the country, a château in Dordogne my father had left me, and we spent a fair amount of time there. Bernard ran up a shocking amount of bills, but that's another story. He would have ruined me, if I'd let him, but fortunately my father's attorneys exercised some control. Under pressure from them, I told him eventually that I would no longer pay his bills. He would have to be responsible for them himself, and he got very angry. I discovered afterward that he was in debt for several million dollars, and in order to spare us both the scandal, I settled them quietly for him.

'We were in Dordogne that summer.' She stopped for a moment, fighting for her composure, as Marie-Ange braced herself for what would come next. 'Charles was with us . . .' Her voice nearly drifted away to nothing, and then she went on. 'He was four. And beautiful and blond. He still adored Bernard, although I was slightly less enchanted by then, and terrified by his debts.' It rang an instant chord with Marie-Ange, as she listened to what the woman said, and her heart went out to her as she spoke of her child. 'There was a fire one night, a terrible fire. It devoured half the house before we discovered it, and I ran to find my son. He was in his room, above us, and the housekeeper was out. And when I got there, I found Bernard . . .' her voice was barely more than a croak, 'locking Charles's door from the outside. I fought with him, and tried to unlock it, he had the key in his hand. I hit him and took it, and went after him myself, and when I got Charles out of his bed, I couldn't get through the door again. He had blocked it with something, a piece of furniture, a chair, something. I couldn't get out.'

'Oh, my God . . .' Marie-Ange said, as tears slid slowly down her cheeks, and she pulled Robert closer to her heart. 'How did you get out?'

'The firemen came and held a net beneath the window. I was afraid to drop Charles into it, and I held him in my arms. I stood there for a long time, afraid to jump.' She cried harder as the memory flooded her, but she was determined to tell Marie-Ange, no matter how agonizing it was. 'I waited too long,' she said, choking on the words, 'my son was overcome by the smoke and died in my arms. I was still holding him when I jumped. They tried to revive him, but it was too late. And Bernard was pulled out of the main floor, completely hysterical, and claiming that he had been trying to rescue us the entire time, which was a lie. I told the police what he had done, and of course they checked, and there was nothing blocking the door to my son's room. Whatever he had put there, he had removed after I jumped, and before he got out. He told the police that I was unable to accept the hand of fate in the death of my son, and that I had to blame someone to exonerate myself. He sobbed endlessly at the inquest, and they believed him. He said I was unbalanced, and had an unusual and unnatural attachment to my son. And they believed everything he said. There was no evidence to support my story, but if he had killed us, he would have inherited everything my father had left, and he would have been a very, very rich man. The firemen discovered later that the fire had started in the attic, they said it was electrical, and one of the wires that ran through there was badly frayed. I believe that Bernard did that, but I cannot prove it. All I know is what I saw him do that night, he was locking Charles's door when I arrived, and he blocked the room so we could not get out. All I know, Comtesse, is what happened, what I saw, and that my son is dead.' Her eyes bored holes through Marie-Ange, and it would have been easier and less painful to believe she was crazy, that she had wanted to blame someone, as Bernard had said at the inquest. But something about her story, and the way she told it, made Marie-Ange shiver with terror. And although she didn't want to believe it of him, if it was true, Bernard was a monster and a murderer, as surely as if he had killed the child with his own hands.

'I do not know your situation,' Louise went on,

as she looked at the young woman holding the baby, so obviously upset by what she'd just heard, 'but I understand that you have a great deal of money, and no one to protect you. You are very young, perhaps you have good attorneys, and perhaps you have been wiser than I was in protecting yourself. But if you have left him money in your will, or if you have no will at all and he will inherit automatically from you if you die intestate, you and your children are in grave danger. And if he is dangerously in debt again, the peril is greater still. If you were my daughter, or my sister,' her eyes filled with tears as she said it, 'I would beg you to take your babies, and run for your life.'

'I cannot do that,' Marie-Ange said in a strangled whisper, looking at her, wanting to believe her crazy, but unable to do that. She was distraught over everything she had just heard. 'I love him, and he is my children's father. He is in debt, certainly, but I can pay for it. He has no reason to kill us, or hurt us. He can have anything he wants.' She wanted to believe that the story she had just heard was a lie. But it was not easy to do.

'There is a bottom to every well,' Louise said simply, 'and if yours runs dry, he will desert you.

But before he does that, he will take everything he can get. And if there is more that he can only get if you die, then he will find a way to get that too. He is a very greedy, evil man.' He was worse than that. He was a murderer in her eyes. 'He came to Charles's funeral, and cried more than anyone else there, but he did not fool me. He killed him as surely as if he had done it with his own hands. I will never be able to prove it. But you must do everything you can now to protect your children. Bernard de Beauchamp is a very dangerous man.'

There was a long, agonizing silence in the room as the two women looked at each other for a long time. It was hard for Marie-Ange to believe he was as bad as Louise said, and yet she believed her story. Perhaps she had only imagined that the door was blocked, but there was no explaining why he had tried to lock the child's door from the outside. Perhaps he had hoped to protect him from the smoke and the fire, but even that seemed hard to believe now. Maybe he panicked. Or maybe he was truly as evil as she said. Marie-Ange didn't know what to think or say. She was breathless with shock and grief.

'I'm so sorry about what happened.' There was

no way to console her for all she had lost. Marie-Ange looked at her sadly and then told her what Bernard had said to her. 'He told me you had died with your son. Ten years ago, in fact.' In truth, it had only been five, three since the divorce. 'And he said that Charles was his.'

Louise smiled at that. 'He only wishes I had died. He's very lucky. I don't go out, and see only a few friends. After the inquest, I saw no one for a long time. For all intents and purposes, in his world, I might as well be dead. And there is no point trying to convince people of my story. I know what happened. And so does Bernard, no matter what he says. Be careful,' she warned Marie-Ange again as she stood up. She looked exhausted, and there were still tears in her eyes after all she'd said. 'If anything ever happens to you, or your children, I will testify against him. That may mean nothing to you now, but perhaps it will one day. I hope you never need me for that.'

'So do I,' Marie-Ange said as they walked to the door of the apartment, and the baby stirred.

'Beware of him,' Louise said ominously as they shook hands.

'Thank you for seeing me,' Marie-Ange said

politely, and a moment later, she was walking down the stairs and realized that her legs were shaking, and she was crying for Louise and her son and herself. She wanted to call Billy and tell him what Louise had told her, but there was nothing he could do. All she wanted to do now was run away and think.

It was nearly seven o'clock when she left her, and it was too late to drive back to Marmouton. She decided to spend the night at the apartment in Paris instead, although she knew Bernard was there. She was almost afraid to see him, and all she could hope was that he didn't sense anything different about her. She knew she would have to be guarded about what she said. And as she walked into the apartment, he was just coming back from a meeting with the architect at the rue de Varenne.

The house was nearly ready, and they were saying that it would be finished after the first of the year. He looked happy and surprised to see her, and kissed the baby, and all she could think of as she watched him was the boy who had died in the fire, and the woman with the ravaged face.

'What are you doing in Paris, my love? What a

wonderful surprise!' He seemed genuinely pleased to see her, and she felt suddenly guilty for believing everything Louise had said. What if she was crazy? What if none of it was true, or if she was demented with grief and did in fact need someone to blame? What if she had killed her son herself? The very thought of it made Marie-Ange shudder, and as Bernard put his arms around her, she felt sorrow and love for him well up in her again. She didn't want to believe it, didn't want him to be as evil as Louise had said. Maybe he had told her Louise was dead because he didn't want to tell her of the horrors of the inquest, or Louise's accusations against him. Perhaps there was some reason why he had lied, even if only fear of losing or hurting Marie-Ange, however wrong he'd been. He was human after all.

'Why don't we go out to dinner? We can take the baby with us if we eat at a bistro. You still haven't told me why you're here, by the way,' he said, looking innocently at her, as she felt torn in two. Half of her adored him, and the other half was filled with fear.

'I missed you,' she said simply, and he smiled and kissed her again. He was so loving and so gentle and so sweet as he held the baby, that she suddenly began to doubt everything Louise de Beauchamp had said. The only thing that did ring true was his penchant for running up debts. But that was certainly not fatal, and if she was careful, perhaps in time he would learn to keep it in check. And perhaps he had lied to her out of fear. She felt sure of it as they went out to dinner, and he made her laugh, as he held the baby, and told her some funny piece of gossip he'd heard about one of their friends.

He was so sweet and so loving with her that by the time they went to bed that night, with Robert in the bassinette beside them, she was certain that Louise de Beauchamp had lied to her, perhaps in order to get even with him for leaving her. Perhaps she was only jealous of her, Marie-Ange told herself. Marie-Ange said nothing to him about the meeting, and she felt sorry for the woman she had met, but no longer sorry enough to believe her. Marie-Ange had lived with Bernard for two years, and had two children with him. He was not a man who would murder women and children. He couldn't hurt anyone. His only sin, if he had any at all, Marie-Ange decided as she fell asleep in his arms that night, was that he ran up a few debts. And the lie about his being a widower was one she could forgive. Perhaps, as a Catholic and a nobleman, it had simply seemed too great a sin to him to admit he was divorced. Whatever had been his reason, Marie-Ange loved him in spite of it, and did not believe for an instant that he had killed Louise's son.

Chapter Eleven

Marie-Ange felt so guilty when she went back to Marmouton, after her meeting with Louise de Beauchamp, that she was doubly kind to Bernard when she discovered that he was further in debt. He hadn't said anything to her, but it turned out that he had forgotten to pay for the rental of their summer house and the yacht that went with it, and she had to pay the bill herself. But at this point, it seemed like a small sin to her.

The house on the rue de Varenne was almost finished, and although there were a stack of bills still waiting to be paid, she had finally decided to borrow some money against her trust to pay them off. His investments that had been promising to 'mature' for two years so he could sell them off had never materialized, and she had long since stopped asking him about them. There was no point. She was no longer even entirely sure that they were there. Perhaps he had lost the money, or had less than he said. It didn't matter to her anymore. She didn't want to embarrass him. And they had her trust to live on. They had two beautiful houses, and two healthy children. And although she thought of her meeting with Louise de Beauchamp from time to time, she pushed it out of her head and said nothing to him about meeting Louise. She was sure that the woman had maligned him, and accused him unfairly. It was just too terrible to believe that she actually thought he had killed her child. But Marie-Ange forgave her for what she'd said about her husband, because she was sure that if she had lost one of her children, she would have gone quite mad herself. Bernard and her babies were all she lived for now. And it was obvious to her that Louise de Beauchamp was deranged by grief.

And when Bernard talked about buying a palazzo in Venice, or a house in London, she scolded him now like a little boy who wanted more candy, and told him they had enough houses. He had even talked about going to Italy, to look at a yacht. He had an insatiable appetite for luxurious items and houses, but Marie-Ange was determined to keep an eye on him, and keep his extravagances in check. And by the time Robert was three months old, Bernard was already talking about their having another child. The idea appealed to Marie-Ange too, but this time she wanted to wait a few months longer, although she had already regained her figure and was prettier than ever, but she wanted to have a few months to spend more time with Bernard. They were talking about taking a trip to Africa that winter, and Marie-Ange thought it would be fun. And as Christmas approached, they were planning a big party at Marmouton, and another even bigger one after the first of the year, when they occupied the house on the rue de Varenne.

Marie-Ange was busy with her babies, and she called Billy a few weeks before Christmas to ask about his wedding plans. She wanted to go back to Iowa to visit him, but it seemed so far away, and there was never time. He teased her and asked if she was already pregnant again. But in a quiet moment at the end of the conversation, he asked if she was all right.

'I'm fine. Why did you ask that?' He always had a sixth sense about her, but she insisted she was fine. She didn't say anything about her meeting with Louise de Beauchamp, out of loyalty to Bernard. And she knew it would have been hard to explain, especially to Billy, who was somewhat suspicious of him.

'I just worry about you, that's all. Don't forget I've never met your husband. How do I know if he's really such a great guy?'

'Trust me,' Marie-Ange smiled at the red-haired, freckled memory of him, 'he really is a great guy.' It made her sad to think that she hadn't seen Billy in such a long time. But he was happy for her that she was at Marmouton with her own family. It seemed like poetic justice to him.

'Do you ever hear from your aunt?' Carole was in her eighties by then, and Marie-Ange knew she hadn't been well for a long time. She had just sent her a Christmas card with a photograph of Heloise and Robert, but she didn't think it would mean much to her. She always wrote to Marie-Ange at Christmastime, a terse little note, once a year. And all she ever said was that she hoped that she and her husband were well. She never said much more than that. 'Are you still coming to my wedding in June?' Billy asked.

'I'm going to try.'

'My mom says you should bring your kids.' But it was a long way to take them, and if Bernard had his way, she'd be pregnant again by then, although she could travel anyway. But Iowa seemed like part of another world.

They chatted for a little while, and then Bernard came home, and she got off the phone, and went to kiss him hello.

'Who were you talking to?' He was always curious about what she did, who she saw, who she talked to, he enjoyed being part of her life, although he was sometimes more private about his own.

'Billy, in Iowa. He still wants us to come to his wedding in June.'

'That's a long way off,' Bernard smiled. To him the States meant Los Angeles or New York. He had been to Palm Beach a couple of times, but a farm in Iowa was definitely not his style. He had just bought himself a set of matched brown alligator luggage, and Marie-Ange could just imagine him arriving at the Parker farm with his alligator bags in the back of a pickup truck. But she would have liked to go back, and was still promising herself she would someday. She had tried to talk Billy into coming to Marmouton for his honeymoon, and then going to Paris, and had even offered to let him stay at their new house, but he had only laughed at the suggestion. He and Debbi had decided a week at the Grand Canyon was too expensive, and even a weekend in Chicago would be tight for them. France was a whole other life, and only a dream for them. They put every penny they had into the farm.

'What did you do today, my love?' Bernard asked her that night over dinner. They had just hired a cook from town, and it was nice having the extra time with her children, but she missed making dinner for him.

'Nothing much. I was doing some things for our Christmas party, and some shopping. I played with the children.' Heloise had a cold again. 'What about you?'

He smiled mysteriously at her. 'Actually,' he said, as though waiting for a drum roll to accompany his announcement, 'I bought an oil well,' he said, looking pleased, as Marie-Ange frowned at him.

'You did what?' She hoped he was teasing her, but he looked frighteningly sincere.

'I bought an oil well. In Texas, actually. I've been talking to the people selling shares in it for quite a while. It's going to make a fortune when it comes in. They've had some tremendous luck before in Oklahoma.' He beamed at her.

'How did you buy it?' She felt panic rise in her throat as she asked.

'With a promissory note. I know these people very well.'

'How much was it?' She sounded nervous and he looked amused. 'How much was your share?'

'It was a bargain. They let me pay for half a share now, with the note, of course, for eight hundred thousand dollars. I don't have to pay the other half till next year.' And she knew by now that he never would. She would be responsible for it, and they would have to borrow more against her trust. Two years before, $10,000,000 had seemed like a vast fortune, now she was constantly terrified that they would go broke. In Bernard's hands, $10,000,000 disappeared like dust.

'Bernard, we can't afford it. We just finished paying for the house.'

'Darling,' he laughed at her naiveté, as he leaned over to kiss her, 'you are a very, very rich woman. You have enough money to last forever, and we are going to make a fortune on this. Trust me. I know these men. They've done it before.'

'When do you have to cover the note?'

'By the end of the year,' he said blithely.

'That's in two weeks.' She nearly choked at what he said.

'Believe me, if I could, I'd cover it myself. Your advisers at the bank are going to thank me for doing you a favor,' he said, without batting an eye, and Marie-Ange lay in bed awake, thinking about it, all that night.

In the morning, when she called the bank and told them, her advisers were in no mood to thank Bernard, and for her sake they refused to let her borrow the money against her trust to cover the note. They flatly wouldn't allow it, and at lunch the next day she had no choice but to tell Bernard, and he was enraged.

'My God, how can they be so stupid! And now

what do you expect me to do? My word is my honor. They'll think I'm some kind of liar, they might even sue me. I signed the documents two days ago. You knew that, Marie-Ange. You have to tell the bank that they *have* to pay.'

'I did,' she said grimly, 'maybe we should have asked the bank before you signed.'

'You're not a pauper, for God's sake. I'll call them myself tomorrow,' he said, implying that she had handled it badly. But when he called the trust department, they were even more direct with him, and told him in no uncertain terms that her trustees would not allow her to borrow against the trust again. 'The doors are closed,' they said. And when he talked to Marie-Ange about it, he was furious with her.

'Did you tell them to do that?' he asked suspiciously, accusing her of double-crossing him.

'Of course not. But we've spent a fortune on both houses,' and he had spent another million dollars or more on art and bad debts from other deals. Her trustees had told her that they were protecting her, and what was left of her fortune, for her own good. She had to think of her future, and her children. And if she couldn't restrain her husband, they were more than willing to do it for her. But Bernard was like a caged animal over it for the next several days. He ranted and raved at her, and behaved like an angry, spoiled child, but there was nothing she could do. They sat through meals in stony silence, and by the weekend, when Bernard came back from a brief trip to Paris, he finally sat down with Marie-Ange in his study, and told her that in view of her obvious distrust of him, and her bank treating him like a gigolo, obviously at her direction, he was thinking of leaving her. He was not going to tolerate being treated this way, or living in a marriage where he wasn't trusted, and was treated like a child.

'I have had your best interests at heart since we met, Marie-Ange,' he said, looking wounded. 'My God, I let you stay here when I didn't even know you, because I knew how much it meant to you. I spent a fortune restoring the château because it's a relic of your lost childhood. I bought the house in Paris because I thought you deserved a more exciting life than being hidden away here. I have done nothing but work for you, and for our children, since the day we met. And now I discover that you don't trust me. I cannot live this way anymore.' She was horrified by what she was hearing, and even more so at the thought of losing him. She had two small children, and she might be pregnant again. The idea of his leaving her, and leaving her alone in the world again, with her children, filled her with terror, and made her want to give him everything she had. It also never occurred to her that the expensive restoration he was claiming, she had actually paid for herself, or that the 'fortune he had spent' was hers. She had paid for the house in Paris, after he had bought it without even asking her before he made the commitment, just as he had committed to the promissory note for $1,600,000 now, without ever asking her.

'I'm sorry, Bernard . . . I'm sorry . . .' she said miserably, 'it's not my fault. The bank won't lend me the money.'

'I don't believe you even tried. And it *is* most certainly your fault,' he said harshly. 'These people work for you, Marie-Ange. Tell them what you want. Unless of course you want to humiliate me publicly, and refuse to cover a debt I entered into for you. You're the one who would benefit from this investment, as would Robert and Heloise.' He was everything self-sacrificing and noble as he accused her, and she felt as though she had shot him in the heart. And in return, he was breaking hers.

'They're not my employees, Bernard. They're my trustees, you know that. They make the decisions. I don't.' Her eyes implored him to forgive her for what she couldn't give.

'I also know that you can take them to court, to get what you want, if you want to.' He was the image of injured virtue as he explained it to her.

'Is that what you want me to do?' She looked shocked.

'If you loved me, you would.' He had put it all on the line, but the next day, after Marie-Ange spoke to the bank again, they still refused, and when she threatened them with court, they told her in no uncertain terms that she would lose. They could point out easily how quickly and how recklessly her money had been spent, and they told her that no responsible judge in the world would overturn the trust under those circumstances, for a girl her age. She was only twenty-three, and they knew how grasping Bernard would look in those circumstances, and how suspicious to the court, but they did not say that to her.

And when she reported the conversation to Bernard, he said coldly that he would let her know what he decided to do. But she had been warned. He had already threatened to leave her if she did not cover the debt. And it was a matter of less than two weeks before he had to pay.

She was still beside herself over it the night of their Christmas party, and Bernard hadn't spoken to her in days. He felt humiliated and mistrusted and abused, and he was making her pay for it in spades. And she looked very nervous as she greeted their guests. He looked, as always, elegant, dignified, and cool. He was wearing a new dinner jacket he had had made in London, and a pair of custom-made patent leather shoes. He was always exquisitely dressed, and she was wearing a red satin gown he had bought her at Dior. But she felt anything but festive, and she was worried sick that he would leave her by the end of the year, when she couldn't cover his debt. He acted hurt that she didn't feel he was doing everything for her.

He said not a word to her as they led their guests into the dining room for dinner, and later on when the music struck up, he danced with every woman in the room, save his wife. It was a painful evening for Marie-Ange, in every way.

And all but the last guests had left, when someone in the kitchen commented that they smelled smoke in the house. Alain Fournier, their caretaker, was washing dishes in the kitchen, and helping the caterers clean up, and he said he'd take a look around to see what it was. At first the caterers insisted it was the oven they were cleaning, and someone thought it might be the candles lit throughout the house, or the cigars the guests had smoked. But just to be on the safe side, Alain wandered upstairs to look around. And on the second floor, he found a candle that had leaned too far toward the heavy new damask curtains. The tassels on the curtains had caught fire quickly, and one whole side of the curtains was on fire when he came upstairs.

Alain tore it off the rod, threw it on the floor, and stamped it out, but only then did he notice that the row of fringe at the top of the curtains had carried the flames to the other side, and now they were blazing too as he began to shout, but no one heard. He tried desperately to put the fire out before it spread any further, but because of the music downstairs, his cries for help were drowned out, and like a nightmare, the flames danced from one curtain to another, and within what seemed like instants, the entire second-floor hallway was on fire, and the flames were darting toward the stairs.

And without knowing what else to do, he rushed back downstairs to the kitchen, and told them to bring buckets and water and come upstairs to help, as one of the caterers ran to call the fire department, and then into the living room to warn the remaining guests. And the moment Marie-Ange heard it, she ran upstairs, heading for the second floor hall, where Alain was throwing water at the flames. By the time they got there, the fabric on the walls leading from the second floor to the third had created a tunnel of flame, but she knew she had to go through it, since both her children were asleep upstairs. But as she attempted to pass through the flames, powerful arms held her back. The men who had come up from the kitchen to fight the fire knew she would turn into a human torch in her billowing red dress, as the walls blazed.

Danielle Steel

'Let go of me!' she said, screaming at them, and trying to fight her way past them. But before she could wrench herself free of them, she saw Bernard run past her, and he was already at the top of the stairs as she pushed free of the men and ran up the stairs as quickly as she could behind him. She could see the door to the nursery just ahead of them, and the hallway was already full of smoke, as she saw him pick the baby up and then run into the room where Heloise was sleeping in her own crib. Heloise woke the moment she heard her parents, and Marie-Ange reached down and grabbed her. They could hear the roar of the fire by then, and downstairs she could hear people shouting. And as Marie-Ange looked behind her, she saw the stairs to the third floor alight with flame, and she knew that the windows on the third floor were tiny. Unless they could get back downstairs through the flames, there would be no escaping, and she looked at Bernard in desperation.

'I'll get help,' he said, looking panicked, 'you stay with the children. The firemen are coming, Marie-Ange. If you have to, go to the roof and wait there!' And then, he set Robert down in

Heloise's crib and made a dash down the stairs, as Marie-Ange watched him in terror. He stopped for only an instant on his way down, at the door to the roof, and as she watched him, she saw him slip the key to the door into his pocket, and she screamed after him to throw the key back to her, but he only turned once at the foot of the stairs, and vanished, gone to get help, she was sure, but he had left her alone on the third floor with her babies, in a sea of flames.

Bernard had told her he didn't want her to try to get through the flames on the stairs, she was safer waiting upstairs, he'd said. But as she watched the flames drawing closer to them, she knew he was wrong, and it was small consolation as she heard sirens in the distance. Both her children were crying by then, and the baby was gasping in the thick smoke that had begun to choke them. She was expecting to see firemen, or Bernard with a bucket brigade, coming up the stairs to save them at any moment. She couldn't hear the voices downstairs anymore, the roar of the fire was too loud, and a moment later she heard an enormous crash, and when she looked, she saw that a beam had fallen and was blocking the stairway. And there was still no sign of Bernard coming back to them, as she sobbed, and held both her babies.

She put them in Heloise's crib for a moment, and ran to check the door to the roof, but it was locked, and Bernard had taken the key with him. And suddenly she remembered a voice in her head, and a scarred face, and everything Louise de Beauchamp had said to her. It was all true, she realized instantly. He had tried to lock them in her son's room. And now he had left her here, with no access to the roof, and no way to escape the fire and save her children.

'It's all right, babies. It's all right,' she said murmuring frantically to them, running from one small round window to another, and then as she looked out one of them, she saw him standing there, down below in the courtyard, sobbing hysterically and waving his arms in their direction. He was describing something to the people below, and shaking his head, and she could just imagine now what he was saying, perhaps that he had seen them dead, or that there was no way for him to get to them, which was true now, but it hadn't been when he left them, and slipped the key to the roof into his pocket.

She opened all the windows she could, so they could breathe fresh air, and then rushed from room to room as embers fell and pieces of flaming wood flew all around them. And suddenly, she remembered a tiny bathroom they never used. It was the only room on the third floor with a slightly bigger window, and when she got to it, she saw that it could open. She rushed back to Heloise's room and grabbed both of them, and then rushed back to the bathroom and began screaming from the open window.

'Up here! I'm up here! . . . I have the children!' She screamed above the din, waving one arm out the window, and at first no one saw her, and then suddenly a fireman looked up and noticed her, and ran quickly for their ladder. But as she watched the men below, she saw Bernard look up at her with a look she had never seen on his face before. It was a look of pure jealousy and hatred, and she had no doubt at that moment that he'd done this. He had set the fire probably, on the second floor, where no one would notice, close enough to the stairs to the third floor so that it would devour his children. And he had known what Marie-Ange would do, she would go to them, and be trapped with them.

It was no accident of hysteria that the door to the roof was locked, he had taken the key with him. He had wanted to kill them. And from what she could see, there was a good likelihood that he would succeed. The firemen had put their ladders to the walls of the château, and found they would not reach up far enough for them to reach her. And as Bernard watched, he began to sob hysterically, just as Louise had described the night her son died. Marie-Ange felt a chill of terror rush over her, she could not see how she was going to save her children. And if they all died, Bernard would inherit everything, if they lived and Marie-Ange didn't, he would have to share the estate with his children. His motive for killing all of them was a thought so disgusting and unbearable that Marie-Ange felt as though her chest had been torn open and her heart ripped out. He had tried to murder not only her, but their children.

And as she looked below and watched him cry, she held the children as close to the window as she dared, to keep them breathing. The door to the tiny bathroom was closed behind them, and the roaring sound from beyond it was deafening. She couldn't hear what anyone was shouting to her from below, but three of the firemen were holding a net for her, and at first it was not clear what they were saying. She watched their mouths as intently as she could, to read their lips, and finally one of the men held up a single finger. One, he was saying to her. One. One at a time. She sat Heloise down on the floor at her feet, as the child clung to her dress, and sobbing hysterically, she kissed Robert's tiny face, and held him out as far as she could, as the firemen rushed beneath her and held the net firm. It was an unbearable moment as she let go, and watched him fall and bounce into the net like a little rubber ball, and then finally she watched one of them as they held him. But he was still moving. He waved his arms and legs as Bernard rushed to him, and took him in his arms, as Marie-Ange looked down at him with hatred.

And then she did the same with Heloise, while the child kicked and screamed and fought her and Marie-Ange shouted at her to stop, and then kissed her and threw her. And like her brother, she fell into the net like a doll, and was grabbed by the firemen, and then kissed by her father. But they were all looking up at Marie-Ange now, as she stared out the window. It had been one thing to throw them, another to leap from the window herself. It looked like an agonizingly long way down, and the window was so small, she knew it would not be easy for her to climb through. But as she looked at Bernard in the courtyard below, she knew that if she didn't, he would have her children, and God only knew what he would do to them, to steal their share of the inheritance. She knew from that day forward, they would never be safe with him. She climbed to the windowsill, and sat poised, as she heard an explosion downstairs and all the second-floor windows blew out into the night, and she knew it was only a matter of time before the floor beneath her gave way, and collapsed, taking her with it.

'Jump!' the firemen shouted at her. 'Jump!!' But she felt frozen as she sat there, and they were powerless to help her. There was nothing they could do for her, except encourage her to do what she had done for her children. And as she sat, clutching the window frame, she could see Louise de Beauchamp's face in her mind's eye and knew what she had felt that night, when she had lost her son, and had known that Bernard had killed him, as surely as if he had taken a gun and shot him. If nothing else, Marie-Ange had to leap to save her own children from him, and to stop him. But it was so terrifying she couldn't move. She was paralyzed with terror as they watched her.

She could see Bernard screaming to her, her babies were in other arms than his by then, and all eyes were turned toward her. And knowing that no one was watching him then, Bernard looked up as he hung back in the crowd and smiled at her. He knew she was too frightened to do it. He would gain the lion's share of her estate when she died, and he could do anything he wanted with it once he had it. He had failed in his mission to kill his last wife, and killed only her son, but this time he would be more successful. And the next time, Marie-Ange wondered as she looked at him, who would he kill then? Heloise? Or Robert? Or both of them? How many people would he destroy before someone stopped him? And as though she were next to her, Marie-Ange could hear Louise speaking of Charles the night he died in her arms in their country house, and it was as though Louise spoke to her now, loudly and clearly.

'Jump, Marie-Ange! *Now!*' And as she heard

the words in her head, she leaped finally from the window, and flew down, her big red skirt billowing like a parachute, and it knocked the wind out of her when she landed in the net they held for her. The first face she saw looking down at her was Bernard's, crying and holding his arms out to her, as she shrank from him. She had seen it all in his eyes before that, she had understood everything. He was truly the monster Louise had said he was. He was a man who had been willing to kill her child, and his own, and two women. And as Marie-Ange looked at him, she spoke clearly.

'He tried to kill us,' she said calmly, stunned by the sound of her own voice, and the words she was saying. 'He took the key to the roof with him, after he locked it, so we could not get out. He left us there to die,' she said, as he stepped backward as though she'd hit him. 'He's done it before,' Marie-Ange said for all to hear, but he had tried to destroy all that she held dear, and she would never forgive him for it. 'He set a fire that killed his last wife's son,' she said, as rampant hatred leaped from his eyes toward her. 'He locked them in a room as well, and nearly killed her, but he didn't. You tried to kill us,' she said directly at him, as he reached out as though to slap her and then stopped himself, fighting for composure.

'She's lying. She's insane. She's always been unbalanced,' and then he tried to sound calm, as he spoke to the fire chief standing next to him, listening, and watching Marie-Ange's face. She didn't look unbalanced to him. 'She's come unglued from the shock of seeing her children in danger.'

'You set the fire, Bernard,' she said to him in an icy tone. 'You left us there. You took the key. You wanted us to die, so you could take all the money, not just mine, but theirs too. You should have died in the fire, and perhaps next time you will,' she said as the rage she felt began to boil over, and the local constable moved toward Bernard discreetly. One of the firemen had said something to him, and he was suggesting to Bernard that he come with them and answer some questions. And Bernard refused to go with him, and expressed his outrage.

'How dare you! How dare you listen to her! She's a lunatic! She has no idea what she's saying.'

'And Louise? Was she a lunatic too? And what about Charles? He was a four-year-old child when you killed him.' Marie-Ange was sobbing by then, as she stood in the freezing night and one of the firemen put a blanket over her shoulders. They had nearly stopped the fire by then, but the destruction inside the house was almost total.

'Monsieur le Comte,' the constable said clearly to him then, 'if you do not come with us willingly, sir, which I hope you will, we will be obliged to put you in handcuffs.'

'I'll see that you're fired for this. It's an outrage!' he objected, but went with them. Their friends had long since departed, and Marie-Ange was left with the caretaker, the men who had come up from the farm, the firemen, and her babies.

They had given oxygen to Robert, and he was shivering, but calm by then, and Heloise was fast asleep in the arms of a fireman, as though nothing had happened. Alain offered to let them stay with him that night, and as she watched the last of the fire burn, Marie-Ange realized that once again she was starting from nothing. But she was alive, and she had her children. That was all she cared about now.

She stood outside for a long time, as the firemen continued to put out the last of the fire, and they stayed all night to watch the embers. She took the children into the caretaker's cottage with Alain, and in the morning two policemen came to the door and wanted to see her. Alain's mother had come up from the farm shortly before that, to help her with her children.

'May we speak to you, Comtesse?' they asked discreetly, and she stepped outside with them. She didn't want Alain to hear what she had to say about her husband. They questioned her extensively, and told her that the firemen had found traces of kerosene in the second-floor hall, and on the stairs leading to her children. There would be a full investigation made, and as things stood now, they were prepared to bring charges against Bernard. She told them then about Louise de Beauchamp, and they thanked her.

She took a room for herself in a hotel in town that night, and they set up two cribs for her children, and Madame Fournier came with her. She was there for a week, to answer questions for the police and firemen, and after the fire cooled, she went back into the house to see what could be saved. Some silverware, some statues, some tools. Everything else had been destroyed or ruined, but the insurance people had already been there to see it. There was some question as to how much or if they would pay her anything, if it could be proven that Bernard had set the fire himself.

And she called Louise de Beauchamp after the first few days. It took Marie-Ange that long to calm down. The aftermath of the shock was worse than what she had felt the night it happened. She had lost not only her home, and nearly her children, but her hopes, her dreams, her husband, and her faith in him. He was being held in the local jail for further questioning, and Marie-Ange hadn't been to see him. All she wanted was to ask him why he had done it, how he could have hated her so much, and wanted to destroy their babies. It was something she knew she would never understand, but his motives were clear. He had done it for money.

And when they spoke on the phone, Marie-Ange thanked Louise for her warning. Had she not known, perhaps she would have been foolish enough to believe he was coming back for her, and never tried to find her way out through the bathroom window. And certainly, she would have believed his histrionics. But she would never forget seeing him that night, and the look of hatred in his eyes, as he watched her poised on the windowsill, praying she wouldn't dare leap to safety.

'I thought I heard your voice that night, telling me to jump,' Marie-Ange said sadly. 'I was so afraid to, I almost didn't. But I kept thinking of what he would do to them if I died . . . and then I heard your voice in my head, saying "jump," and I did.'

'I'm glad,' Louise said quietly, and reminded Marie-Ange that she would gladly testify to what had happened to her, and Marie-Ange told her the police were going to call her. 'You'll be all right now,' Louise reassured her, 'better than I. Poor Charles was sacrificed to that bastard's greed. What a terrible thing to die for.'

'I'm so sorry,' Marie-Ange said again, and they talked for a long time, comforting each other. And in a way, Marie-Ange knew, Louise's warning had saved her, as much as the firemen and the net they had held, and the leap of faith she had taken.

They spent Christmas in the hotel, and the day after, Marie-Ange drove the children to Paris. She had already decided to sell the house on the rue de Varenne, and everything in it. She hated to stay in the apartment, but all their things were there, all that they had left, and Bernard could no longer hurt her. He had tried to call her once at the hotel, and she had refused his call. She never wanted to see him again, except in court, and she hoped he would go to prison forever for what he had done to Charles, and tried to do to her children. But the real tragedy for Marie-Ange was that she had not only trusted and believed in him, she had loved him.

It was New Year's Eve when she finally called Billy. She was at home with her babies, and thinking about him. She had so much to think of, values and ideals, and dreams that had been destroyed, integrity that had never existed. Like Louise, she realized now that she had been nothing more than a target for him from the first, a source of funds that he would have bled till it ran dry. She was just thankful that her trustees had been more cautious than she was. But at least the sale of the house in Paris would restore some of her financial balance.

'What are you doing at home tonight?' Billy asked when she called. 'Why aren't you out celebrating? It must be midnight in Paris.'

'Pretty close.' It was shortly after, and it was five

in the afternoon for him. He had been planning to spend a quiet night at home, with his family and his fiancée.

'Aren't you supposed to be at a grand party somewhere, Countess?' he teased her, but she didn't smile. She hadn't smiled in almost two weeks.

She told him about the fire, and what Bernard had done, or tried to do. She told him about Louise, and Charles, and the money Bernard had bilked from her. But more than anything, she told him what it had felt like, in the bathroom during the fire, and throwing her children out the window, and as he listened to her, she could hear him crying.

'My God, Marie-Ange, I hope they send the son of a bitch to prison forever.' He had never trusted him. It had all happened so quickly. Too quickly. And Marie-Ange had always insisted that everything was so perfect, and for a while she thought it was. But now that she looked back, she realized it never had been. She even wondered if the children he wanted so desperately had only been a way to distract her and tie her to him. She was just grateful now that she hadn't gotten pregnant a third time, but since the fire, she had been reassured that she hadn't. 'What are you going to do now?' Billy asked her, sounding more worried about her than ever.

'I don't know. The hearing is in a month, and Louise and I are both going to be there.' She had described her face to him, and the tragedy she'd been through. Marie-Ange had been a great deal luckier in being able to save her children. 'I'll be in Paris until I figure out what to do. There's nothing left at Marmouton. I suppose I should sell it,' she said sadly.

'You can rebuild if you want to,' he encouraged her, still trying to absorb the horror she had told him, and wishing he could put his arms around her. His mother had seen him crying on the phone, and had shooed everyone out of the kitchen, including his fiancée.

'I'm not even sure I do want to,' Marie-Ange said honestly about the home she had loved as a child, but so many tragedies had happened there that she was no longer sure she wanted to keep it. 'So many awful things happened there, Billy.'

'Good things too. Maybe you need to take some time to think about it. What about coming here to kind of catch your breath for a while?' The idea appealed to her immensely, although she didn't want to stay at a hotel, and she couldn't impose two small children on his mother. Everyone on their farm was busy and had their hands full.

'Maybe. And I can't come in June for your wedding. I have to be here for the lawyers, and they said he might go to trial then. I'll know later.'

'So will I,' he said, smiling, and looking more boyish than ever, although she couldn't see him. Marie-Ange was twenty-three, and he was twenty-four now.

'What does that mean?' Marie-Ange questioned his cryptic comment.

'I don't know. We've been talking about putting the wedding off for another year. We like each other a lot, but sometimes I wonder. Forever is a hell of a long time. My mom says not to rush it. And I think Debbi's kind of nervous. She keeps saying she wants to live in Chicago. You know what it's like here. You're not talking big-city excitement.'

'You should bring her to Paris,' Marie-Ange said, still hopeful it would work out for them. He deserved happiness. She had had her turn, and it had literally turned to ashes. Now all she wanted was peace and some quiet times with her children. It was hard to imagine ever trusting anyone again, after Bernard. But at least she knew Billy, and loved him as her brother. She needed a friend now. And then she had an idea, and proposed it to him. 'Why don't you come to Paris? You can stay at my apartment. I'd love to see you,' she said, sounding homesick. He was the only person in the world she could trust now.

'I'd love to see your kids,' he said, thinking about it.

'How's your French these days?'

'I'm losing it. I have no one to talk to.'

'I should call more often.' She didn't want to ask him if he could afford the trip, or insult him by offering to pay for it, but she would have loved to see him.

'Things are pretty quiet here right now. I'll talk to my dad. He could probably get by without me for a week or two. We'll see. I'll think about it, and see what I can work out.'

'Thank you for being there for me,' Marie-Ange said with the smile he remembered so well from their childhood.

'That's what friends are for, Marie-Ange. I'm always here for you, I hope you know that. I wish you hadn't lied to me about him. Sometimes I thought something was wrong, and other times you convinced me you were happy.'

'I was, most of the time, a lot of the time, really. And my kids are so sweet. But he scared the hell out of me the way he spent money.'

'You'll be okay now,' he reassured her, 'the main thing is that you and the kids are fine.'

'I know. What if I lend you the money for a ticket?' she asked, worried he didn't have the money and afraid to embarrass him, but she was dying to see him. She suddenly felt so scared and so alone, and so lonely, and it felt like a hundred years since she'd seen him. It had been just over two, but it felt like decades. And so much had happened. She'd gotten married, had two kids, and nearly been destroyed by the man she'd married.

'If I let you lend me the money for the ticket, how would you be able to tell me from your husband?' He was serious. He didn't want to do the same thing to her as Bernard, but he couldn't even conceive of the scale on which he'd done it.

'Easy,' she laughed in answer to his question, 'just don't buy an oil well with the money.'

'Now there's an idea,' he said, laughing at her. He thought she was kidding. 'I'll figure out what I'm going to do, and I'll call you.'

'I'll be here,' she said with a smile, and then remembered. 'And by the way, Happy New Year.'

'Same to you, and do me a favor, will you, kid?'

'What's that?' It felt like their old school days just talking to him.

'Try to stay out of trouble till I get there.'

'Does that mean you're coming?'

'That means I'll see. Just take care of yourself and the kids in the meantime. And if they let him out of jail, I want you to fly out here.'

'I don't think that's going to happen. Not for a long time,' but it was a sensible suggestion, and she was grateful for his concern.

After they hung up, Marie-Ange got into bed. Heloise was sleeping next to her in her bed, and Robert was in his crib in the next room. And she smiled to herself as she thought of Billy.

At that exact moment, he was talking to his father. Tom Parker had been more than a little startled by the question, but he said that he figured maybe he could spare it, as long as Billy eventually repaid it, and Billy promised to do that. He had been saving for their honeymoon and already had $400 put aside.

But when he walked back into the living room, his sisters thought he looked distracted. One of them spoke to him and at first he didn't even hear.

'What's with you?' his oldest sister said, as she handed her baby to her husband.

'Nothing much.' And then he told them all what had happened to Marie-Ange, and they were horrified. His fiancée, Debbi, was listening with interest, but said nothing. 'I'm going to Paris,' he said finally, 'she's had a hell of a time, and it's the least I can do, for old times' sake.' It was impossible for any of them to forget that she had given him his Porsche.

'I'm moving to Chicago,' Debbi spoke up suddenly and silenced the room as they all stared at her.

'Where did that come from?' Billy asked her, and she looked embarrassed.

'I've been waiting all week to tell you. I found a job, and I'm moving.'

'And then what?' he asked, feeling a strange

flutter in his stomach. He wasn't sure yet if he was glad or sorry, mostly confused, but he had been for a while, when he thought about their wedding.

'I don't know yet,' Debbi answered honestly, as his entire family listened. 'I don't think we should get married,' and then she added in a whisper, 'I don't want to live on a farm for the rest of my life. I hate it.'

'That's what I do,' he said quietly, 'it's who I am.'

'You could do something else if you wanted,' she whined at him, and he looked unhappy.

'Let's talk about this outside,' he said calmly, and handed her her coat, and they walked out onto the porch, as the rest of the family began to chatter. They still couldn't believe what he'd told them about Marie-Ange, and his mother was worried about her.

'Think they'll ever get married?' his older sister asked her about Debbi.

'God knows,' their mother said with a shrug, 'damned if I know what people do, or why they do it. The ones that should get married, don't. The ones that shouldn't can't wait to run off with each other. Most people make a mess of it, if you give 'em half a chance. Most of them anyway. A few don't, like your dad and I,' she said, grinning over at her husband, who was still intrigued by what was going on around him.

And when Debbi left, Billy went straight to his room, without explaining anything to his parents or sisters or brothers, or their respective spouses. He said nothing at all, and softly closed the door.

Chapter Twelve

When the plane from Chicago landed at Charles de Gaulle, Marie-Ange was waiting for it, with Robert in her arms, and Heloise in the stroller. She was wearing slacks and a warm coat and heavy sweater, and her babies were bundled up in matching little red coats that reminded her of her childhood. And she was holding a single rose for Billy.

She saw him as soon as he got off the plane, and he looked just the way he always had when they rode to school on the school bus. Except he wasn't wearing overalls, he was wearing jeans, a white shirt, and a heavy jacket, and brand-new loafers his mom had got him. And he sauntered toward her just the way he always had, when she waited for him on her bike, in the places where they used to meet and talk during the summer. And he smiled the minute he saw her.

Without saying a word, she handed the rose to him, and he took it and looked at her for a long moment, and then he hugged her close to him, and felt the silk of her hair on his cheek, as he always had. It was like a homecoming for both of them, they were each the best friend the other had ever had, and even after two years, it was old and comfortable and sure that they loved each other. It was the way things ought to be, and seldom were. It was the same way Françoise had felt the first time she saw John Hawkins again when she saw him in Paris, but neither of them knew that. And after Billy had hugged her, he stopped to look at her kids. They were both beautiful, and he said they looked just like her.

And as they walked toward the baggage claim, she told him how the first hearing had gone. They were charging Bernard with three counts of attempted murder, and they were reopening the investigation about the death of Charles, Louise's son. The prosecutor said that given the new evidence against him, it was more than likely

Danielle Steel

he would be charged with murder.

'I hope they hang him,' Billy said with a vehemence she didn't remember about him, but he couldn't stand thinking about what she'd gone through. And he had had a lot of time to think about it again, on the plane, and before that, when Debbi moved to Chicago. They had finally agreed to break their engagement, but he hadn't told Marie-Ange yet. He didn't want to scare her. She might be worried if she thought his engagement was broken off.

Billy had come for two weeks, and she wanted to show him all the sights in Paris. She had planned the whole trip for him, the Louvre, the Tour Eiffel, the Bois de Boulogne, the Tuileries, there were a thousand things she wanted to show him. And then they were going to drive down to Marmouton, just so he could see it, but they couldn't stay there. They would have to stay at the hotel in town, and then drive back to Paris the next day. But she wanted to walk the fields with him at least, and show him the orchards, and get his advice about whether or not he thought she should rebuild it. But if she did, she wasn't planning to put in any of the excessive luxuries

Bernard had. She wanted it just like the old days, when her parents lived there. And maybe in the end, it would be a good place for her and her children. She hadn't made up her mind.

When Billy picked up his small bag off the turntable, she looked at him and saw that he was different. He was more grown-up, more confident, more at ease with himself. He was a man now. And she had changed too. She had been through a lot, and she had two babies. She'd been through the wars with Bernard, and come through them eventually. And now Billy was here, and in the best possible ways, nothing had changed, as he looked down and grinned at her, as he took the baby from her with one arm, and she pushed the stroller.

'It's like coming home again, isn't it?' She looked up at him with a smile, as he said it, and he smiled at her. She saw something flicker in his eyes and asked him what he was thinking. They had always read each other's minds.

'I was just thinking that I'm damn glad you jumped out that bathroom window. I would have had to kill him myself, if you hadn't.'

'Yeah, me too, I'm glad I jumped, I mean.' She

smiled, as they walked along, looking like a family. There was no reason for anyone to guess they weren't. The four of them looked right together. And all Marie-Ange wanted now was to be with him for the next two weeks, and talk about all the things they always had, and that meant something to them. They had lives and dreams and secrets to share, things to talk about and explore. And Paris to discover. It was as though a door was closing behind them, and another was opening right before them, into a brand-new world.

THE END